Swedish Gem

Tom Walton

Tom Walton

ISBN: 978-1-63491-041-5

Published by BookLocker.com, Inc., Bradenton, Florida.

Printed on acid-free paper.

BookLocker.com, Inc.
2015

First Edition

"Never draw to an inside straight.
Never bet a filly against a mare."

\- *Harvey Volk Walton*

Dedication

To Sherilyn, my wife of 35 years.
They said it wouldn't last.

Prologue

Stephanie Shafer tries to look interested as she leans against the front of her classroom desk listening to 21 eighth graders talking about their upcoming spring break plans. She glances at the clock almost as often as her students do counting down the last five minutes before the 3:15 bell rings. Stephanie, however, has another kind of ringing bell on her mind. If she can just get on a winning streak and win $5,000 at the local casino tonight, she can pay the loan shark enough to enjoy her seven-day cruise to the Caribbean with her husband Tony knowing the next 'day of reckoning' won't happen for another three weeks.

The last round of "going skiing," "just babysitting," and "playing video games" echoes around the classroom as she fills the last few minutes of this Friday afternoon having students announce their spring break plans. The bell finally rings. Stephanie uncrosses her arms and ankles, pushes herself away from the desk, brushes bangs off her face, and gives knuckles to all the boys and girls as they already hastily start parading by. The room quickly empties with one final "Have a nice spring break, Mrs. Shafer." Stephanie nods, drops her smile before it drops her, and digs into her purse to see how much cash she has in her billfold for the evening. Finding eight crisp $100 bills, she smiles and says quietly, "I will indeed, kiddos. I will indeed."

Out of habit Stephanie gathers her briefcase full of papers from the desk to take home for the week. She has no intention, however, of grading them over spring break. After all, Tony and she by Sunday afternoon will be aboard a cruise ship heading to the Yucatan Peninsula for seven days. She takes one last walk around the classroom inspecting desks and checking for left behind jackets and such. She turns out the lights and then quietly leaves the room quickly locking the door.

"Looking good, Steph," Carl Phillips, the 250-lb. balding math teacher from the classroom across the hall, says as he heads out the building at the same time as her. About two inches shorter than Stephanie's 5′8″, Carl struggles to keep up with a suddenly and deliberately rushing Stephanie. He almost trips in his EEE loafers trying to match her pace.

"Thank you, Mr. Phillips," Stephanie acknowledges with little expression and no eye contact. She quickens her pace toward the door refusing to be any more familiar with him than possible. She also doesn't want to outwardly show that she enjoys the compliment. Three sessions at the *All about U* salon has tanned her slim 28-year-old body enough for her to look forward to spending plenty of time in a bikini sunning on the top deck of the cruise ship. She knows she looks good. With each step toward the parking lot and away from Mr. Phillips her walk transforms Mrs. Shafer, the attractive middle school teacher, to Stephanie, the bouncing barracuda of casinos near and far.

A quick check of her cell phone as she gets into her silver Honda Accord indicates no missed calls or texts. That leads to a relieved sigh and a big smile. She checks herself out in the mirror, likes what she sees, but decides that to complete her makeover for the cruise she will add blond streaks to the bangs of her shoulder-length auburn-colored hair and a two-inch layer of purple along the bottom.

"See you in nine days, Steph." Mr. Phillips manages to make it to his car, but it takes all he has to trek the 50 yards to it parked in the faculty lot. He always makes it a point to park next to Stephanie as often as he can, even though she subtly parks farther and farther away to deter his idle flirting. Stephanie gives him a quick wave without turning around and heads toward home with a feeling that maybe lady luck for Tony and her might be ready to change for the better.

Three blocks down the street she passes the school bus. One of the boys sticks his head out of the window, waves, and blows a bubble the size of a grapefruit. Stephanie gives him a wave and wink as she passes. Other students see her and wave and holler out the windows of the school bus. She shakes her head, gives a wry chuckle, and enters the ramp to the interstate.

American Woman followed by *No Time* rocks at full volume on *The Guess Who Greatest Hits* CD playing in her car as she drives across town. She loves classic '70s rock music much to the chagrin of Tony who thinks otherwise. Stephanie's dad had been a disc jockey in college on an FM stereo rock radio station back in those days. He instilled in her a belief that the post Beatles '70s were, indeed, the real golden age of rock 'n roll.

She cruises down the interstate to the singing of Burton Cummings and the guitar riffing of Randy Bachman, her dad's favorite rock stars. She happily anticipates good times ahead and tries to place on the back burner her two very real and very pressing problems.

Another spring break has finally arrived. This one will be different, though, since Tony and she will be spending the week on a cruise ship, something they have never experienced

She continues driving northeast slightly above the speed limit toward the state line between Oklahoma and Arkansas thinking about everything she has to do to get ready for the trip in the morning. Now including stopping by the hair salon, the drive reminds her of the first time she had been on this road.

1

Stephanie and Tony had moved to Arkansas five years ago when he received an offer with a sizable raise to work for his uncle who owned a series of franchised restaurants across the state. It took a lot of talking for Tony to convince Stephanie to leave the southeast Oklahoma area where she had grown up. But she finally relented when she drove to the Arkansas River Valley to check out Fort Smith during a three-day weekend while Tony went on a golfing road trip with his co-workers. It also gave her a chance to visit her parents who lived in Tulsa, less than a two hour drive north northwest.

Stephanie's parents, Harry and Martha Snyder both nearing retirement age, had just heard the news that their other daughter Rachel, four years older than Stephanie, had suffered a second miscarriage. Rachel had not stopped smoking and drinking during her pregnancies. Two bad habits she had started doing heavily during high school. According to her doctor, in each instance nicotine had crossed her placenta and interfered with the blood supply to the fetus. He also said that some of the environmental toxins associated with her living and working on a rundown farm had an adverse effect, as well. The fact that her husband Jimmy Brooks and she frequently smoked marijuana and dabbled with cocaine clearly played a role, too. The doctor had told her several times that in her particular instance, if she intended on ever having a successful pregnancy, then she would have to stop smoking, drinking, and "whatever else you may be doing to pollute your system." He strongly advised moving away from the farm on which she and Jimmy lived. Rachel had tuned out the doctor's recommendation just as she had ignored the same message first from her parents and since almost constantly from Stephanie.

Rachel and Jimmy lived in the small town of Cedar Crest, less than an hour drive east from her parents who had moved from hometown Durant to Tulsa after Stephanie entered college. Harry and Martha feared Rachel and Jimmy might ask if they could move in with them. Not what the elder Snyder's desired at all being still bitter about Rachel running off with Jimmy the night of high school graduation to get married.

Rachel's troubles had taken a toll on her parents. She had been a problem child from the start of her school years frequently getting in trouble during elementary school for her "unruly manner and general lack of respect" as her principal described her on more than one occasion to her parents. In junior high she got suspended for vandalism of school property. In high school she got suspended for both smoking on campus and showing up drunk for class.

When Stephanie strongly objected to Rachel's sudden eloping to marry Jimmy Brooks that night eight years ago, Rachel considered that the last straw and declared a permanent splitting of the sheets between the two of them. Stephanie thought Jimmy no good and seldom hesitated to scold Rachel for her latest bad choice.

Jimmy's parents had long been divorced, gone their separate ways, and had no contact with him or his two brothers. As dysfunctional as the Brooks family was, Stephanie feared Rachel's medical issues were placing too much stress on her aging parents, stress they did not need and stress about which Stephanie would try to alleviate.

No longer willing to give any emotional support or financial assistance to Rachel and Jimmy, Harry and Martha had washed their hands of her and their "worthless" son-in-law. Although Stephanie was concerned mostly about her parents, she also couldn't give up on her big sister for fear she would get dragged so far into the world of Jimmy and his dysfunctional family that she could never recover.

Stephanie had been helping Rachel financially for the past two years. Despite the differences that always kept a wedge between the two sisters, the most recent being Jimmy's apparent lack of emotional support for Rachel's pregnancy issues, Stephanie still felt the need to help her out. Harry and Martha didn't know about the money, and Stephanie intended to keep it that way. The possibility of living less than a two-hour drive from her parents in Tulsa played a role in Stephanie considering a move to the Arkansas River Valley.

***

As Stephanie approached the Arkansas state line that day five years ago she noticed familiar sites that fueled an instant adrenaline rush. Sure she had already developed a gambling problem rationalizing her habit to help pay for Rachel's medical bills, but she had no idea so many casinos dotted the highways so close to the Arkansas border. "Hot damn, I think I can live here after all."

She pulled into the parking lot of one of the casinos just on the Oklahoma side, took out her cell phone, dialed Tony's number, and excitedly waited for him to pick up. "Tony, Tony, Tony, we are moving to Arkansas."

"Oh, really, Steph, what brought this on?"

"I'm sitting in the parking lot of a big casino. Why didn't you tell me? They're everywhere."

Tony took the phone away from his left ear, looked at the phone quizzically and then moved it to his right ear. "Why didn't I tell you what? Where are you?

"I told you, I'm in the parking lot of a casino, one of many around here, apparently. Take the job."

"Whoa, girl, wait a minute. What are you doing there?"

"I didn't have anything to do while you're with your golfing buddies for the weekend, so I thought I'd check out Arkansas to see if I could live there."

"That's great news, hon. I'm glad to hear it."

"I figured it would be. Listen, I'm going in for just a bit. Then I'm checking out the city for malls."

Before Tony could say anything else, Stephanie clicked off her phone. She didn't want anything to spoil her giddiness, not Tony's golf stories or his warnings to her about not spending too much time or money in the casino, a message she has grown tired of hearing. She parked between two cars both with Arkansas plates and headed in.

As she entered through the double doors she noticed an off-track betting room (OTB) to her right on the level below. It reminded her of her dad who loved to play the horses. "Never bet a filly against a mare," she whispered, one of the fatherly pieces of advice she remembered from him.

To the left she could see and hear all the familiar sights and sounds of rows and rows of slot machines like "her" casinos back in the Durant area. When she exited the elevator on the casino level a poker room caught her eye. "Never draw to an inside straight," came to mind, another piece of advice from her dad.

She walked by the High Limits room, now feeling warm with a bit of nostalgia. Resisting the temptation to go in for only a walk around to check out the slot machines, she headed in the other direction for the center of the casino in search of the table games pit. It didn't take her long to find it.

A Roulette table anchored the near end of the pit, and a Craps table anchored the other. She perused the pit noting two Ultimate Texas Hold 'em tables (aka UTH, for short), a Three-Card Poker table, and a Mississippi

Stud table mixed in with six Blackjack tables of various minimum and maximum betting limits from $2.00 to $100. The UTH table on the far side didn't have any empty seats available, but the one on the other side sat empty. An attractive young lady dealer with short red hair and freckles stood smiling cheerfully with two decks of cards, one blue and one red, fanned across the table in front of her. "Hi, would you like to play? I've got plenty of open seats."

Stephanie stopped and smiled looking closely at the dealer's name tag. "Polly," she said. "I don't like to play heads up."

"I understand. Sit down. I bet someone will come by pretty quick."

"Well, why not," Stephanie couldn't resist. "Besides, I've never been here before. I've got some questions."

"No problem." Polly picked up the two decks of cards and began shuffling. "Welcome and good luck."

Stephanie once again soaked in all the addictive sounds and sights as she opened her purse and pulled out two

$100 bills. "My husband has been offered a job in Fort Smith. I'm here checking it out."

"What do you think about it so far?" Polly cheque-changed Stephanie's cash into four green $25 chips, 19 $5 red chips, and 10 yellow $.50 chips for antes.

"I haven't made it into the city yet. I drove from Durant and saw this place, thought it might make for a nice pit stop."

Polly dealt the first hand. "Oh, so you play at the casinos around there?"

"You might say that." Stephanie laughed. She turned over her cards revealing an ace and king of spades. "Big slick suited on the first hand."

The hand did not pan out, neither did the next one and the one after that. Stephanie lost her $200 in less than five minutes. She headed for the nearest ATM machine.

***

Six weeks later, Stephanie and Tony had packed all their things, piled them in his truck and her car, said "so long" to southeast Oklahoma, and headed toward the Arkansas River Valley. Talking on their cell phones for the first hour of the three-hour drive, they discussed getting married, buying a house, and having a baby. They made a quick stop for gas and a restroom break at yet another travel plaza that happened to have a small casino attached. Instead of going in to play slots for a bit, they settled instead for buying a handful of chocolate bars and Diet Dr. Peppers. It seemed that little casinos grew like weeds all along the route, but no time for that now. During the next phase of the drive Stephanie in her car happily sang along to some old Bee Gees CDs thinking about soon becoming Mrs. Stephanie Shafer. Tony in his truck thought quietly about his now unofficial fiancé and her mounting gambling debt.

***

Tony had gotten Stephanie started gambling eight years ago while they attended Southeastern Oklahoma State University in Durant. She needed to find a means to make enough money to help Rachel whom she knew would struggle, her running away to marry the no-good

Jimmy Brooks farm boy with neither of them knowing "come here from sic 'em" about what was in store for them.

Stephanie's part-time work study job in the campus bookstore provided little more than pocket money. She did, however, have an accessible savings account thanks to her parents' generous gift to her upon graduating high school.

To say the Brooks clan Rachel married into lacked any semblance of decency would be an understatement. How she got hooked on Jimmy in the first place had always been a mystery to Stephanie. Rachel, however, resented any disparaging talk about Jimmy, choosing to nip any concerning conversations between Stephanie and her with a contentious, "Someday you'll understand, but until then just let it go. I mean it kid."

Stephanie and Rachel's parents had expressed enough displeasure, disappointment, and frustration with Rachel growing up that Stephanie knew something was bound to happen someday that would lead her parents to severing all ties with Rachel. Stephanie took that as enough justification to chip away at her savings account to finance what she considered moderate gambling as a way to ensure always being there for Rachel. Disagreements or not, arguments or not, Stephanie and Rachel were sisters.

Tribal casinos in southeast Oklahoma became Friday night havens for both Stephanie and Tony during their last year of college. Since the finish line to their four-year marathon had gotten closer and closer, they felt they deserved to begin indulging in weekend activities of a more adult persuasion. Tony favored the Blackjack tables. Stephanie got quickly hooked on the Ultimate Texas Hold 'em table game.

They had been a couple since freshman year when they worked together on a group project in speech class. Tony had asked her to a mixer dance, and they started dating steadily right away. By the middle of their sophomore years, they had left the dorms and moved in together in a basement apartment down the street from campus and not far from the house where Stephanie had grown up.

Her first night at the casino she got quads (four of a kind) on her second hand and a full house on her third hand. Playing five dollars on the trips (three of a kind) or better bonus bet her quads paid 30-1 and her full house paid 8-1. Suddenly in less than five minutes she had won $190 just on bonus bets alone not including her winnings from just playing the hands.

A handsome man with a short-cropped haircut wearing a purple oxford cloth shirt with a flashy purple and yellow-striped tie that hung perfectly to the top of the beltline of his gray slacks entered the pit area and checked the player ID display on each table. When he got to the UTH table he noticed that Stephanie did not have a player's card. "Welcome, young lady, would you like a Player's Club card?"

He introduced himself as William Riggs, explained to Stephanie all the benefits of having a Player's Club card, and topped it off by offering to comp a buffet if she played for at least an hour. Rachel told him that she was here with her boyfriend Tony Shafer. "He's the guy in the hoodie and ball cap at that blackjack table," Stephanie pointed across the pit.

William looked over to where she pointed. "He looks like a nice enough fellow. I think I can arrange for both of you to eat dinner tonight."

With that Stephanie handed over her ID and in a few minutes had a Player's Club card and a voucher for two buffets. As the evening progressed, a player at her table got a royal flush which paid at 500-1, a total winning of $2,500 for a five dollar bet in addition to $250 for the 50-1 five dollar bonus bet. That plus hearing the announcement from the players club booth every hour listing all the jackpot winners of $1,200 or more the last 60 minutes, easily hooked her onto the rush of "adult gaming."

Friday night visits soon became Friday and Saturday night visits as the winning sessions began to increasingly outnumber the losing nights. Points more rapidly accumulated on their various players' club cards they had accumulated from every casino in the area. In less than a year they had obtained VIP status at each area casino entitling them to free rooms, free meals, free show tickets, and free gifts. Tony always felt his gambling habit to be well under control. Stephanie's attitude, though, concerned him. He sensed her becoming thoroughly addicted.

Time spent at the casinos increased. Time spent on her studies decreased. Reading about table game strategies took up more time. Reading about Bloom's Taxonomy and other jargon common for secondary education majors to learn took up less time. As a result, Stephanie's senior year at Southeastern home of the Savage Storm got a bit stormy for her. Tony had his girlfriend's (and hopefully future wife) gambling addiction to worry about, a problem Stephanie did not see at all.

Fall semester flashed by as Monday through Friday on campus became not much more than filler time between weekends at the casinos. Friday and Saturday evenings had evolved into all-nighters with free rooms to sleep in during the day. Five dollar bets with red chips at the tables had turned into $25 dollar bets with green chips. But the real storm brewed when the temptation to play slot machines finally blew Stephanie away. "I can't believe all these people sitting at those silly machines hour after hour throwing their money away," Stephanie had said to Tony during one of their early visits.

"I know. They're all hoping for pie-in-the-sky."

"Yeah, right," Stephanie rolled her eyes. "You never know. That next spin could be the big one." They laughed, shook their heads, and headed for the main pit hoping for a seat at one of the tables.

"Good evening, Stephanie." Casino host Dorothy greeted her that Friday night before Halloween weekend. "Would you and Tony care to dine in the steakhouse this evening?"

William, the table games supervisor, had recommended to the casino host supervisor that Dorothy take on the duties of making sure Stephanie and Tony always enjoyed their time at this casino more so than at any others in the area. Dorothy favored the younger couples and enjoyed helping ensure that these special guests of hers felt so special that they would easily advance to higher levels of patronage. The more Stephanie and Tony played, the more points they earned on their Player's Club cards, and the quicker they moved up from copper to silver to gold to platinum to diamond-level status. The higher the status, the bigger the perks and the more frequent the comps.

"Sounds great," Stephanie answered smiling as big and genuine as Dorothy.

"Any specials tonight," Tony asked

"Yes, Mr. Shafer we're having prime rib and rib-eye specials as well as grilled Mahi-Mahi with a mango salsa."

"I'm up for it," Stephanie smiled.

"Lead on," Tony said as he put his arms around both of them.

Stephanie and Tony had finished tests earlier in the day and definitely felt pumped for a celebration marathon at what had become their weekend home away from home. The cold late autumn wind blowing outside certainly added to the need to stay indoors.

Tony, a math major, had breezed through his tests. He knew he had aced them. He had a knack for numbers. He had even become a decent card counter at the Blackjack tables. He looked forward to graduating in May with a 4.0 GPA. Stephanie, on the other hand, had struggled to stay focused all semester. She hoped she had managed to not blow her low 'A' average she had struggled to maintain all fall. If she fell into the 'B' zone, though, it didn't concern her. Her desire to match Tony's 4.0 GPA no longer mattered. The only numbers that concerned her now had hearts, diamonds, spades, and clubs on them.

All she had left for the rest of the fall semester were capstone projects which consisted of an oral presentation reviewing what she had learned in her four years of classes. Having a knack for talking and presenting herself charmingly, she worried not a bit about what all her classmates called "the dog and pony show."

Spring semester would be her 'practice teaching' internship at nearby Soper, a small K-12 school district 45 miles to the east of campus. Since Tony and she lived together in an apartment on the east side of Durant, the drive would not involve dealing with much traffic. It could have been worse. One of her former roommates got assigned to Fort Towson, another 30 minutes farther east.

After a delicious meal of a medium rare 12-ounce rib-eye with a loaded baked potato and a side of sautéed leeks for Tony and the grilled Mahi-Mahi with mango salsa accompanied by a side of steamed broccoli in a light cheese sauce for Stephanie, they headed for what had become their usual suite on the top floor of the hotel. All this comped, of course, as would be breakfast and dinner at the buffet the next day.

Over the course of a year they had graduated from having an occasional regular-sized room on the lower floors with a free deck of cards waiting for them on the night stands to having a choice between either a penthouse or a suite on the top floors with gift bags waiting for them on the coffee tables of the living room. One week the bag contained fluffy white terry cloth bathrobes and slippers to take home, another week a warm throw afghan with a bottle of champagne. Other weeks they received tickets to Dallas Cowboys, Dallas Mavericks, or Texas Rangers games or even clubhouse passes to PGA golf tournaments played in the Fort Worth and Dallas area. Other gifts included hoodies in the winter, t-shirts and ball caps in the summer, and free gas cards year round. This particular Friday night, the gift bag contained not only his and her black leather jackets, but a note.

> *Dear Stephanie,*
> *You and Tony are my most special and appreciated patrons. I am pleased to inform you that you both have $1,000 in free slot play added to your Player's Club cards. You may redeem them on any of our slot machines starting tonight through midnight December 31. Thank you both for your patronage and especially for your warmth and kindness. Always let me know anything I can do for you.*
> *Sincerely,*
> *Dorothy*

"What the hell," Stephanie giggled, "It's free play, let's do it."

Tony gave her a cautious look, waved his finger, and warned, "Be careful, Steph, once you start playing those one-armed bandits you'll end up losing everything you've ever won on the tables plus a whole lot more. You know how you are."

"Don't be silly," she scoffed, "It's free play. Anything we win is money on the house."

"Why do you think they would give each of us $1,000 of free play? Once you get started and win some, you're going to get even more hooked."

"Lighten up, I don't hear you objecting to it." Stephanie made a good point. Tony enjoyed playing the casinos as much as she did. He knew, however, that all the gifts and special treatment were just a way of making sure they kept coming back. There was nothing free about them. Stephanie did not see that side of the casino experience. And that greatly concerned him.

They headed down the elevator to the walkway into the casino with Tony as guarded as an over-protective father and her as giddy as a school girl. For the first time Stephanie took in the sounds and sights of the casino from a different perspective. No longer headed straight for the table games as she had done for over a year, she walked briskly through the casino eyeing every slot machine. She stopped to watch anytime she heard bells ring or saw lights flash. Suddenly her disdain for what she had once called "those silly machines" became a quest for "money on the house."

She became instantly fascinated by a machine that caught her attention when the screen above its tumbling symbols lit up red and a bell rang. The lady playing the machine rubbed the red screen with both hands and the symbols tumbled without her hitting the play button or pulling the lever on the side.

On the first spin a single line that looked like a stick of gum appeared all in a row on each of the tumblers. The bell on top of the machine rang again. On the second spin a double line that looked like two strips of gum appeared all in a row on each of the tumblers. The bell kept ringing. The lady shouted, used her left fist to punch the arm of the man sitting at the machine next to her, continued rubbing the red screen with her right hand, but still didn't push the play button or pull the lever. The symbols tumbled again. This time a red seven appeared on the first reel, a square-shaped symbol with a goofy-looking duck on it appeared on the second reel, and another one of the duck symbols appeared on the third reel. Suddenly, the screen where the symbols had been tumbling turned gray and a bunch of lines of text appeared. The lady jumped out of her seat screaming.

"Too bad all three symbols didn't match this time," Stephanie said to a man standing next to her who had also stopped to watch the machine. She hadn't noticed that three other people had gathered around her. They all laughed.

"Honey," the man standing next to her said, "she got two lucky ducks and a seven playing max bet on a five dollar machine. She just won $1,200 on that spin."

"You're kidding me."

"Nope, its paperwork time for her."

"Paperwork, what do you mean?"

"Anytime you win over $1,200 on one spin the casino has to file a 1099 form to the IRS," the man explained. "She's got more coming to her counting what she won on the first two bonus spins."

"Bonus spins?" Stephanie said confused, but intrigued.

"Never played slots before, eh?"

Stephanie shook her head, "I'm strictly a card player at the tables."

"Well, little lady, let me tell you about these machines. Every once in a while on a winning spin the screen lights up red. When it does you get one, two, or three free spins. It's usually when you get three spins that a big win hits. The first spin is usually not too big, the second spin usually a bigger win, and the third spin usually the biggest."

Listening intently Stephanie nodded her head, "I see, but all the symbols didn't match. How could that last spin be a bigger win than the other spins where all three symbols matched?"

"Lucky Ducky is wild. You get one it doubles your win. You get two it quadruples your win. Since she got a red seven on the first reel, then that's the second highest paying symbol."

He pointed out the pay table to Stephanie as the winning lady, now talking on her cell phone, sat waiting for a slot tech to come to the machine with the paperwork for her to fill out. The slot tech told the lady she would return in a few minutes with her payout. "I'll be right here," said the lady. "I'm not going anywhere."

The floor worker did indeed return in a few minutes with a supervisor to witness and verify the payout. Watching the lady receive 12 crisp $100 bills, Stephanie had seen and heard enough to decide she had found a form of adult gaming entertainment to occasionally lure her away from the table games.

Since players occupied all the machines on that row, Stephanie continued her walk around the casino in search of other Lucky Ducky machines, hopefully with an empty seat at one of them. She made her way up and down the aisles seeing machines of all denominations from a penny to five dollars. Some had three reels. Some had five reels. All had different sights, sounds, and symbols. She saw machines based on TV shows, Greek and Roman gods, every animal imaginable, fairy tales, cartoon characters, movie stars, and even aliens from outer space. She saw several rows of Lucky Ducky machines, but none with empty seats until she wandered into a room in the center of the casino she had never even noticed before.

She saw an empty seat at a Lucky Ducky machine mixed in with machines called Mr. Money Bags, Polar High Roller, and Crazy Cherries. Stephanie had found the High Limit room. Hearing lots of bells ringing, she thought she had found the ultimate means to pay all of Rachel's medical bills and save that marriage. She plopped down at a $10 machine with no inkling that she had just gotten caught up in a whirlwind that Tony and she would not begin to escape from for the next eight years.

***

Settled now in the their new digs in Arkansas, Stephanie subbed for a semester before getting her current job teaching eighth grade English in nearby Spiro, Oklahoma. After graduating from Southeast Oklahoma University and well before the move to Arkansas came about, she had gotten hired to teach English to seventh through 12th graders in the small town of Soper, thanks to her impressive practice teaching internship. She stayed one year but not really happy with the low-key lifestyle of the small town or the gossip circulating about her liberal lifestyle. She got a better offer from Fort Towson schools, another small school district, to just teach eighth and ninth graders. She stayed there two years still maintaining an active and closely-scrutinized relationship with Tony. He had landed a job after graduation working as a teller at the First National Bank in Hugo, a small town about hallway between Soper and Fort Towson.

During those times Stephane and Tony could seldom eat in any of the local restaurants or shop in any of the little stores in any of these small towns without suddenly becoming the topic of small talk. Since they also did not regularly attend any of the area churches, they carried the burden of gossip wherever they went. While nobody ever said anything directly to them, disdainful attitudes came through loud and clear on the residents' faces and their hushed comments to each other.

Now being only about three hours from their hometown in Durant and less than two hours from Stephanie's parents and Rachel made the decision to move to Arkansas a lot easier. That plus the fact that several casinos sat just across the state line within 30 minutes of where they worked and lived. Stephane and Tony had bought a modest 1,600 square foot house in a new neighborhood on the southeast portion of Fort Smith halfway between Spiro and his office on the east side of the city. They took less than two weeks to unpack and settle in before getting married.

Their wedding consisted of gathering one of Stephanie's teacher friends and her father, an interdenominational preacher, one of Tony's work friends with whom he played golf, and all heading to the downtown river park at lunch time on a Friday afternoon for a quick ceremony. With the sun shining brightly, a breeze blowing briskly, and the Arkansas River flowing quietly in the background, they held hands under a maple tree and exchanged vows and rings in the presence of their two witnesses.

In less than 15 minutes Stephanie and Tony happily drove off as legally married as if they had planned a big wedding and fretted over what kind of centerpiece should adorn the tables at the reception hall and who should man the guest book. They stopped by Cedar Crest for an awkward visit with Rachel and Jimmy on their way to the Tulsa International Airport. Before catching a flight to New Orleans for a quick honeymoon, they also had a pleasant dinner with Stephanie's parents at the airport.

2

Smiling about that and other recent memories, Stephanie returns to the moment deciding to pack for the cruise before heading to the casino. Those eight crisp $100 bills burn a hole in her purse, but the anticipation of the cruise wins her over … for the moment. Their plans include getting an early morning start to a leisurely 11-hour drive to New Orleans Saturday instead of flying as they had for their honeymoon with the idea of arriving in time for a supper of oysters and gumbo at Drago's in Metairie, a suburb just north of New Orleans. Char-grilled oysters has become a ritual for them ever since their first visit to the "Big Easy" on their honeymoon. Mealtimes when they visit alternate between Drago's and Acme Oyster House or Court of

Two Sisters, a charming outdoor eatery in the French Quarter.

By 7 p.m. Stephanie jams her suitcase to the hilt, manages to get it closed, and preps her carry-on bag. Tony, on the other hand, plans to pack in the morning. While his suitcase sits empty stuffed in his closet, Stephanie's bags sit by the door ready to go. She has made arrangements for a neighbor to feed her cats every morning and scoop their litter boxes every night. Another neighbor has agreed to pick up their newspapers and mail. Tony hasn't even bothered to fill the gas tank of his truck yet, plenty of time for that in the morning. He did, however, have the oil changed and tires checked earlier in the week.

The free cruise, won by Stephanie at the casino, has cost them over $1,000 so far. First of all, neither of them had passports. They cost almost $200 each. Passengers cannot board the ship without one, and they receive strongly repeated suggestions in each email message they get from the cruise line to carry them each time they go ashore in case something happens and they miss the boat before it sails from port – "a rare, but possible occurrence," they are advised.

The cruise line, Swedish Cruise Adventures (SCA), began sending emails the day after Stephanie signed them up for the spring break dates on the Gem. This newest and largest of the ships in the SCA fleet will take them, over 3,000 other passengers, and over 1,500 crew and staff members on a seven-day adventure out of New Orleans with four stops along the Caribbean: Cozumel, Mexico; Belize City, Belize; Roatan Island, Honduras; and back up to Costa Maya, Mexico. Frequent emails encouraging guests to reserve their excursions in advance always contain assurances that sound a little like warnings that if passengers participating in booked, ship-sponsored excursions arrive back at the ship late, the ship will not sail without them. If, however, passengers venture out on their own and arrive late, the ship will leave them behind; thus the need to carry passports.

Secondly, the 'free' cruise means a small cabin on a lower deck below the water level. But when those emails begin, irresistible offers to upgrade to above-the-water-level, larger staterooms promising to "enhance the visual experience and convenience of your time on the ship" convince them to add another almost $200 to the tab for what turns out to be a cabin one deck up with 15 extra square feet of floor space and a round porthole about the size of a basketball. Thirdly, in addition to port fees and taxes of nearly $400, it will cost $16 a day to park Tony's truck in a secured lot across the street from the terminal. Add to that the cost of spending the night in a New Orleans hotel.

By the time Stephanie makes it to the casino Tony has already been at a Blackjack table for an hour to the tune of being nearly $300 to the good. He greets Stephanie with a wave and smile. "Let's pay for this 'free' cruise tonight and then some."

Tony and everybody in the pit who knows Stephanie compliments her on the newly-added color highlights in her hair. She acknowledges them graciously and tells Tony, "Sounds good to me." She gives him a thumbs up and a wink.

Finding a seat at the $5 UTH table, Stephanie's evening with a money mission begins. She hands those eight crispy $100 bills to Marty the dealer who cheque-changes them into a stack of 32 $25 green chips. "So, we're playing green tonight?"

"Absolutely." Stephanie hails a cocktail waitress for her first drink of the evening. "Need to pay for the 'free' cruise.'"

"All righty then." Marty deals the first hand to her and the other three players at the table. "Good luck, let's have some big wins tonight."

The other players, Friday night regulars, have their red $5 chips in play. Stephanie sits at first base, the seat at the end of the table to the left of the dealer. Faith and Doc a married couple who play close to the vest and seldom stay at the tables longer than two hours, sit at the next two seats. J.J., a tire salesman with a scraggly beard and shoulder-length brown hair that has a white streak across the front sits at third base, the seat at the other end of the table opposite Stephanie. J.J. usually plays all evening not leaving until about 2 a.m. He smokes at least a pack of cigarettes and drinks at least a dozen beers during his Friday night forays.

Stephanie catches a pocket pair, albeit only deuces, on the first hand. "Oh my, I got a pair of ducks to start my winning streak."

Marty adds the familiar poker phrase. "Deuces seldom loses."

She pushes four $25 chips onto the play bet. "Think I'll slam them."

"Of course you are," chimes Faith. "Good luck."

She and Doc both have an ace, hers with a suited five and his with an off suit seven. Danny stares at a jack and queen of clubs. "I'm going to wait for the flop," he decides.

Marty turns over his first three cards: an ace, a jack, and a deuce. "Hey," shouts Danny, "Trips for you, Steph, and a pair for all of us."

"Won't that be something if another deuce comes up," laughs Doc.

The three players place their bets and Marty turns over a six and a four. No help for anyone. Marty's pocket cards, a ten and another six, give him a qualifying hand of a pair as the dealer so everyone wins. Stephanie's three deuces collects $225 dollars for her green-chip bets and each of the other three players win a pleasant $20.

Stephanie gives a wave and a smile to Tony at the Blackjack table. He doubles down on 11, draws a ten and collects $50 as his dealer turns over a nine to add to his 15, a bust. He smiles back and points to his ever-growing stack of green chips that now totals over $400. He lifts his bottle of Coors Light. She lifts her just received frozen margarita. They toast each other's good fortune from across the pit.

As the evening goes on an eerie feeling begins to hover over Stephanie like a dark cloud forming in the distant sky heavy with rain. She senses being watched to the point of rubbing the back of her neck to fend off the stare of somebody. Between hands she turns around to see if anybody lurks in the background, but all looks innocent enough to her. Still, she can't get it out of her head that somebody has an eye on her. "How much longer until you change cards?" she asks Tommy, the latest dealer. "I really need to take a break and walk around for a bit."

"Floor," hollers Tommy, "How much longer until we change cards?"

Ricky, the pit boss for the evening, comes over to the table in response to the call from the dealer. "About ten more minutes." He looks at Stephanie. "Are things going that badly?"

Stephanie plans to use the opportunity to walk around the casino keeping alert in case somebody, in fact, follows her. "No, I just need to stretch my legs."

Tony, in the meantime, moves from the Blackjack table to the Craps table. He takes his over $500 winnings for the evening and decides to play some "hard way" bets.

With a funny look on her face that Ricky and everybody else at the table notices, Stephanie adds unconvincingly, "Need to check on Tony, anyway, I haven't heard much shouting from that end of the pit."

Stephanie manages to win two more hands in the ten minutes before time comes to change cards. Now up over $1,000, she leaves her chips on the table to keep her seat and walks the casino to see if she can spot somebody. She just has a feeling. After three laps around the floor including a brief visit to the ladies room, she stops to talk to Tony. "I swear somebody's watching me. It's strange, but I just know it."

"Don't be silly, Steph," Tony assures her. "It's just your imagination. Now go sit down and win some more money."

He kisses her on the cheek, pats her on the behind, and goes back to his business just in time to see a hard eight come up. Stephanie hugs him as the dealer pushes his winnings over to him. As soon as she settles back into her seat at the UTH table with her back to the Craps table, Tony cashes in his chips. He looks around suspiciously knowing that not one but two somebody's watch them. Tony hopes Stephanie and he can make it to the cruise without anything happening, but her revelation worries him that tomorrow morning might not come soon enough, and when it does, they might not be the only couple heading down the same road to the New Orleans port authority on the Mississippi River to catch a cruise ship out of the country.

Tony can't sleep. He tosses and turns in bed. He walks the house. He plays a golf game on the computer before finally giving up about 3:20 a.m. to curl up on his chair in the den. They had stopped playing about 11 p.m. to go to the 24-hour restaurant in the casino located next to the sports bar. They shared a late night breakfast called a full house. It consists of a plate of two fried eggs, two strips of bacon, two sausage patties, two orders of hash browns, and two biscuits all drowned in thick, white gravy. They left the casino just before midnight. Tony had barely gotten his clothes off and his bed clothes on before hitting the sack for an abbreviated night's sleep so he would be reasonably fresh for the drive in the morning.

Not knowing whether he feels anxious about the cruise or the not mysterious to him men keeping a close eye on both Stephanie and him for the last two weeks, or the after effects of the larger half of the shared full house, he bashes the chair with his fist scaring the cats who have joined him on the nearby ottoman. He gets up and walks into the kitchen stopping by the refrigerator for a drink of iced tea from an open bottle sitting on the top shelf. He decides to let Stephanie sleep until 4 a.m. He sits on the sofa. While waiting for the next 40 minutes to tick by, he finally falls asleep.

***

Tony had developed a mental alarm dating all the way back to elementary school. During summer vacation he always wanted to be the first kid at the local golf course in his neighborhood every morning. He would play all day every weekday until dusk, sometimes walking as many as 45 holes with his buddies stopping only for lunch after whichever nine holes they decided to refuel. Tony's usual meal consisted of a dressed hamburger, curly fries, and strawberry milk shake.

In addition, in high school and college he worked as a weekend morning shift disc jockey at a small AM country music radio station in Durant. So having an internal clock that awakened him at 4:45 every morning for years comes in handy this morning. He awakes from his brief nap when the Grandfather clock in the hallway chimes a three quarter of the hour melody.

***

He walks quietly into their bedroom, sits next to Stephanie snuggled under the sheet fast asleep, and gently nudges her on the shoulder. "Steph," he whispers, "I can't sleep. Let's just get up and go."

"What time is it? It's still dark. Good grief, what's your hurry?"

"I told you. I can't sleep. It's almost five."

"Oh for Pete's sake, seriously." Stephanie pulls herself out from under the sheet. "All right, go ahead and hit the shower while I smoke and drink some Diet Dr. Pepper."

Stephanie stretches and staggers toward the kitchen muttering under her breath all the way. She picks up one of the cats and promptly explains to her what it is like living with a human male. She kisses the cat on the head, places her on the kitchen cabinet, and turns on the faucet in the sink so her "fur person" can drink some fresh, flowing water.

Meanwhile, Tony showers, shaves, brushes his teeth, gets dressed and finally packs. All this before Stephanie makes it back from the patio. She promised to not smoke in the new house. She pulls herself together more quickly than usual, and they leave about 6:30 a.m. Stopping to fill the gas tank and to buy hot coffee and donuts, they head for Interstate 40 and drive southeast in the dark out of town by 6:45 a.m.

A little over two hours later and now in daylight they turn further southeast through Little Rock and Pine Bluff. In less than three more hours they cross the new bridge over the Mississippi River near Greenville, Mississippi.

After a third restroom stop Stephanie takes over the wheel and heads south through Yazoo City and Jackson. A few hours and two more stops later they approach Lake Pontchartrain. "We'll be at Drago's in Metairie in time for char-grilled oysters and a cup of gumbo," Stephanie shouts to Tony over the blaring of the Doobie Brothers CD playing at full blast.

"Sounds good." He shouts back at her. "How 'bout turning down that old '70s crap a tad?"

"Are you kidding me? During *Black Water,* no way. Doobie Brothers are classic and must be played loudly, sweetheart, especially when you're on the road."

"Anything you say, dear."

"OK, Aerosmith coming up next. Steven Tyler is still so hot."

Tony tries to find a comfortable position in the passenger's seat for a quick nap. As he settles in, he glances out the back window, something he has done four times since Stephanie took over the driving.

Sure enough, just over 11 hours after leaving home Stephanie and Tony pull into the crowded parking lot at the Drago's in Metairie. They enter to the aroma of Cajun food and the sights and sounds of a bustling restaurant. Seated upstairs at one of the few empty tables, they enjoy a glass of wine and hot rolls while waiting for their much-anticipated meal. Conversation centers on their drive, particularly their unusual sightings between Greenville and Jackson.

"Can you believe all those funerals processions we saw in Mississippi? Stephanie says. "I mean, really, how weird is that?"

"I know, seven of them within, what, an hour or two?"

"Yeah, and how weird that old black Chevy with those two guys that stopped at the same gas station as us in Dumas and Yazoo City."

After eating two cups of gumbo and two dozen char-grilled oysters, they head for Canal Street in downtown New Orleans, destination the casino/hotel near the riverfront. Tired from the day long drive, they gamble for only about an hour. They head to their room for bed by 10 p.m.

In the morning, feeling refreshed and excited about the cruise, they walk a few blocks to Camp Street for breakfast at The Red Gravy, a local bistro specializing in unique breakfast fares. After having Sicilian egg pie, sans the grits, and plenty of hot coffee, they head back to the casino for an hour at the tables before checkout. At 11 a.m. they drive to Julia Street and follow signs to the terminal parking lot. Even though the ship won't sail until 4 pm. early boarding starts at noon.

Stephanie has her carry-on bag of the usual female travel items in a backpack that she easily manages through the terminal and on to the ship. Tony, however, has the bulkier carry-on that holds a six pack of Diet Dr. Pepper, a six pack of bottled water, two boxes of granola bars, a jar of salted peanuts, and two young adult books he plans on reading; *Mockingjay* and *Insurgent. Mockingjay,* the third installment of *The Hunger Games* trilogy and *Insurgent,* the second installment of the *Divergent* trilogy series Stephanie got him started on after she read the books to help keep up with her eighth graders.

Passengers had been advised in several emails to carry on drinks and snacks to take with them on shore excursions in case they don't want to sample the local cuisine at each port. They also had been advised to carry on a set of clothes, swim suits, and other miscellaneous items for the afternoon since their dropped off luggage may not be delivered to cabins and staterooms until after the ship sails. A week's worth of luggage for 3,000 passengers takes a few hours to deliver ship wide. Besides, since the ship only arrived at 8 a.m. from its last trek, all rooms might not be ready for occupancy until later in the afternoon.

"Welcome aboard Stephanie and Tony from Arkansas," the security agent managing the entry way kiosk says in a thick Eastern European accent as he scans their boarding passes. "Hope you enjoy your week with us on the Gem."

"Welcome aboard folks," says another security agent, this one with a distinct Asian accent. He sprays sanitizer on every passenger's hands. "Rooms will be ready before 2 p.m., so please visit the buffet on deck 12 until you hear the call."

As Stephanie and Tony walk the hall of deck four toward the elevator, an attractive young teenaged girl with a French accent greets them with, "Welcome aboard Monsieur and Madame, please take this elevator to deck 12. After enjoying lunch, please visit the other amenities on decks 12 and 13 until you hear the call to check into your rooms."

Though lugging his carry-on gets more difficult with each step Tony keeps a smile on his face. Stephanie and he enter the elevator with about a dozen other passengers. Once reaching deck 12 another uniformed crewmember, this one a young Hispanic lady, directs them to the buffet. "Please enjoy while we prepare rooms and deliver luggage," she says with a smile and a nod.

As a swarm of passengers enter the buffet, two older Mexican crewmembers playing acoustic guitars sing "Happy, happy, washy, and washy." An even older Mexican woman nods, smiles and sprays sanitizer on everyone's hands. Apparently a series of recent sicknesses aboard other cruise lines ships has motivated extra care to not spread germs on any Swedish Cruise Adventures ships.

"Let's just get a salad, says Stephanie. "I want to be hungry for a nice dinner tonight."

"Agreed," replies Tony. "I'm not really hungry."

He finds a table and puts down the heavy carry on while she heads for the food stations. The buffet stretches from mid ship astern with station after station of selections. Stephanie comes back with a bowl of Waldorf salad and a glass of iced tea. Tony fixes himself a bowl of cucumber salad and a glass of cranberry juice with a shot of orange juice added. He scans the seating areas as if looking for familiar faces similar to the way he had earlier scanned the faces in the terminal. Stephanie gives him a quizzical look. "Looking for someone in particular?"

"Oh, just noticing the variety of ages. I see little kids all the way to retired folks."

"Yeah, I see skinny people, fat people, and all body types in between."

Stephanie and Tony leisurely eat their salads. She takes in the sights of all the people scurrying back and forth from stations to tables. He continues to uneasily scan the buffet looking for two men in particular. Stephanie suggests they next head up to deck 13 to check out the pool. About that time an announcement comes over the public address. "Ladies and gentlemen this is Caroline your Cruise Director. I'm happy to report that all cabins and staterooms have been cleaned and ready for occupancy. Please settle in. Don't forget the mandatory safety lecture at 3:30 p.m. Crewmembers will be standing by to lead you to your gathering place. Welcome aboard. I'll have more announcements for you before we set sail."

Good news for Tony so he can finally unload his carry-on. They head for the elevators. With plenty of smiling crewmembers pointing and nodding all wearing red polo shirts, khaki shorts and white deck shoes,

Stephanie and Tony wiggle their way through the narrow hallway of deck five crowded with frazzled passengers loaded with their various sized carry-ons dangling from their shoulders searching the numbers on the doors for their staterooms. Stephanie and Tony finally spot stateroom door 5572 at the far end.

Compact to say the least, the room does have plenty of shelves, nooks and crannies, and reasonable walk space. The queen-size bed, centered under the porthole, leaves about 18 inches of walk space on either side. Small night stands with two shelves sit on each side. The foot of the bed on each side has just enough room for a small dresser and chair. Stephanie claims the one with drawers, a mirror and a small lamp. Tony claims the one with shelves up to the ceiling.

The entry way has a small bathroom on one side and a closet, mini-refrigerator, and more shelves on the other. The bathroom holds a shower, a vanity with more shelves, and a small cubicle for the commode all of which requires a learning curve to navigate.

Shortly thereafter the announcement comes to attend the safety lecture. It takes 15 minutes to crowd everybody in this group into their designated gathering place. The lecture, however, only lasts five minutes involving just learning how to put on a life jacket and where to go to the life boats in case of emergency. Even so, by the time Stephanie and Tony make it back to their stateroom, their luggage has arrived.

In less than 15 minutes all their gear gets neatly and conveniently stowed here, there, and everywhere. Stephanie even finds a home for the luggage under the foot of the bed. After getting settled she brushes her teeth, washes her hands and face, combs her hair, and touches up her make-up. Tony sits on the bed and surfs with the remote to check out all the TV channels. They then begin their first tour of the ship. While walking through a shopping area the size of a small mall, a series of announcements bellow over the speakers with each one beginning with the same cheery, "Ladies and gentlemen this is Caroline your Cruise Director."

The first announcement tells of a gathering in the Skylight Theatre on deck seven at 10 a.m. tomorrow in which Caroline will take everyone attending on a virtual tour of the ship identifying all the amenities and services available. Free gifts will get distributed to all. At 11:30 a.m. someone nicknamed Always-ready Teddy will inform attendees of sanctioned shops and safe areas to visit while in each port and non-sanctioned shops and not-so-safe areas to avoid. All in the audience will receive a free gift and a map.

The second announcement invites passengers to dine in the two complimentary restaurants on the ship. "The Lineage and Luxulos on deck seven near the mid-ship elevators are your free dining choices," Caroline chimes. "Lineage has a family atmosphere with casual dress encouraged. Shorts are welcome, but not swimming attire. Luxulos offers a more upscale atmosphere with a business casual dress code preferred. No shorts allowed."

Caroline also gives a summary of the other restaurants scattered onboard that require a cover charge and reservations. They include Italian, South American, Greek, and Asian cuisines. All four offer premium steaks, as well. She, of course, also reminds passengers about the daily free offerings of breakfast, lunch, and dinner in the Calypso Buffet on deck 12.

Stephanie and Tony agree Caroline has just enough of a French accent and upper Midwest USA dialect to peg her as Canadian. They enjoy trying to guess the home country of each crew or staff member they encounter, a game they started playing back in college after studying about dialects and accents in a required speech class.

They decide to dine at the more informal Lineage and maybe go for Luxulos the next night. Both restaurants open at 5:30 p.m. Finally making their way to the casino, they closely check it out. It will not open until 6 p.m., so they get a thorough and quiet self-tour of the slot machines and table games. Impressed with the variety despite its small size, they give it the thumbs up and look forward to spending evenings engaging in "adult gaming."

3

By now the ship has set sail. For the next hour waiting for the restaurants to open for dinner Stephanie and Tony stand on the railing of deck 13 at the top of the ship. They enjoy the cool breeze and sights of the shoreline as the Gem sails out of New Orleans down to the mouth of the Mississippi River where it drains into the Gulf of Mexico headed to the Caribbean Sea.

At precisely 5:30 p.m. they head to Lineage and get in a line with other hungry passengers, a line that has already formed and snakes around the corner. Greeted by a maître d with a definite New Zealand accent, Stephanie and Tony step down into a surprisingly fancy-adorned dining area. "If this is the more casual of the free restaurants, I can't wait to see the fancier one," Stephanie says.

"Not bad, not bad at all," agrees Tony.

Seated at a table next to an older couple, Stephanie and Tony check out the menu and strike up a conversation with the usual cruise ship icebreaker, "Where you all from?"

"Wisconsin," the blue-haired lady wearing a knee-length floral cover-up over her swimsuit replies.

"Green Bay to be exact," adds the bald-headed man. "Phil and Dorothy Jameson we are." He extends his hand for Tony to shake. "Nice to meet you kids."

"Where you kids from?" Dorothy then asks smiling.

"Fort Smith, Arkansas, We're on her spring break. That's Stephanie and I'm Tony."

"Oh, a school teacher, how nice," Phil beams. "Our daughter teaches school, too."

From that piece of common ground the next half hour goes by with lots of conversation and plenty of good food, made even tastier since it's free. Stephanie orders surf and turf – a 6-oz. sirloin steak with a small lobster tail - and a cup of French onion soup. Tony opts for the 10-oz. NY strip steak, loaded baked potato, and a salad. As the Jameson's and Shafer's finish their hardy meals, the waiter with a thick Laotian accent hands everyone a dessert menu.

"Oh my goodness, we get free dessert, too," exclaims Stephanie.

"Oh yes, dear," Dorothy says. "We've been on this cruise before. There's dessert every night."

"Well, we'll have to start saving room for it," laughs Tony. "And plan to walk a lap around the ship after dinner every night, too."

"Oh don't worry about it, kids" offers Phil. "You're probably going to gain five pounds this week. So just enjoy it."

"Well, then, I think I'll enjoy the apple pie a la mode." Tony pats his belly. "What about you, Steph?"

"I think I'll enjoy the cherry cheesecake tonight."

"Ah, good choice, good choice," nods the waiter. "Be right back with coffee, too?"

"Sounds good," Stephanie says.

"Same for us," adds Phil.

Both couples exchange pleasantries after dessert and head their separate ways, the Jameson's to the bingo parlor and the Shafer's to the casino. Tony begins his stint at the casino by signing up for the daily Blackjack, slot, and Poker tournaments. Stephanie heads to the cashier's cage to enroll in the $5,000 credit line offer she received in an email. "Play now and pay later" the offer promises, irresistible to any frequent adult gaming enthusiast. She signs the necessary paperwork. The young woman at the window hands her a players' card and with a distinct Serbian accent pleasantly instructs Stephanie to "insert this in slot machines before playing or hand to dealers when at tables."

"Okay, and love your accent. Is your name pronounced So-fee-a?"

Sofija nods her head yes. "Thank you, how nice of you to notice."

Stephanie turns to walk away clutching her players' card with $5,000 credit on it. Sofija adds, "By the way you get free drinks in casino with card, too."

Stephanie heads to the UTH table with a sudden surge of adrenaline. She feels optimistic that by the end of the week the ship's casino will be paying her rather than her paying the casino. Finding the only UTH table full, she lands at the Let It Ride table on the other side of the crowded of the larger of the two pits. This one has a Poker table at one end and a Roulette table at the other with three Blackjack tables and two Three-Card Poker tables in addition to the one each UTH and Let It Ride tables.

Just across from a row of video Poker machines sits another smaller pit perpendicular to the larger one. Anchored by a Craps table on the near end it contains three more Blackjack tables on either side. At the far end sits a long wooden table used for sign-ups to all the daily tournaments and stacks of obligatory brochures about "problem gambling" displayed in all casinos.

Stephanie settles into the only empty seat at the Let it Ride table. She notices a high limit pit tucked in a small room one step up from the rest of the floor space hidden from plain site by a narrow doorway. Neither she nor Tony noticed it when they took their self-tour earlier because there had been black curtains pulled together to make it look like a wall. Curiosity gets the best of her so while the dealer scans her card to approve her request for $600 in chips, she walks over and sneaks a peek. A dealer and a pit worker both turn and smile. The pit worker, a tall middle-aged woman with black hair says with a Greek accent, "Care to play Baccarat?"

"No thanks, just checking it out. What all tables do you have here?"

The dealer, a young Chinese man with a high-pitched voice, points to a $100 minimum Blackjack table, two Poker tables and his Baccarat table. "We also use all tables for Poker tournaments when get many players."

Stephanie waves thanks and heads back to the $5 minimum Let It Ride table to find a stack of green and red chips waiting for her. Two seats have opened on the Three-Card Poker table next to her, but she isn't interested. She has her eye on the UTH table and plans to claim the next open seat. Within 30 minutes a seat opens, but somebody grabs it before she can. Disappointed she gets the attention of a pit worker, "Floor, may I have the next seat at UTH?"

The attractive young Italian pit worker Arturo winks at her nodding his head. With that settled she loses her eighth hand in a row and orders her first free drink of the night, a rum and cola.

Fortune doesn't change and the drinks keeps coming. By the time Tony checks on her after playing in preliminary rounds of both a slot and Blackjack tournament, Stephanie has a red face, blurry eyes and a volume increase to her voice of at least two levels. She requests another $600 in chips from Arturo, who she has been innocently flirting with for the past 45 minutes.

She hasn't had nearly as much to drink as a husky fellow named B.J. who can be heard throughout the casino.

Sitting at the table just to the left of Stephanie, B.J. every time he gets Blackjack or the dealer goes bust jumps out of his chair, throws his arms up in the air and shouts, "That's what I'm talking about."

Around 10:30 p.m. during one of his celebrations his elbow catches the elderly lady sitting next to him right on her jaw. It almost knocks her out. Since a couple of security guards have been hovering nearby with their eyes and ears tuned into him, it takes only seconds for them to approach both B.J. and the woozy lady. She has slumped over with the side of her face lying on the table. The sight of the two security guards leading B.J. away from the tables prompts a memory from three years ago that Stephanie and Tony wishes had never happen

4

The losing streak had reached nearly $15,000 before Stephanie and Tony decided to try to recoup some of her losses the old desperation way – by cheating. They had developed such good relationships with the dealers, pit workers, and many regular players at casinos back home that they thought they could get away with just about anything. They devised two plans. Stephanie would work the tables, Tony the slot machines.

On his first attempt Tony amassed over $30 playing the "grocery shopping" gambit. He walked the aisles of the casino in search of those tickets frustrated players cashed out and left on slot machines after losing down to a few cents. He snatched them up like pulling items off the shelves of a Wal-Mart. He also cashed out any remaining few-cent credits players left on machines. He did this each visit to area casinos and totaled over $200 in less than two weeks. It would take some time, no doubt, but by randomly visiting a number of casinos over time, he could put a dent in Stephanie's debt.

Stephanie, on the other hand, played the "sticky coffee cup" ploy. During a break from playing the tables while decks of cards got changed she would order a cup of coffee and then head for the bathroom to apply some glue stick to her index finger. When play resumed and her coffee arrived, she would hold the Styrofoam cup in such a way that she could dab some sticky on the bottom of it. When the dealer would pay a winning hand to the player at the end of the table with the other players looking in that direction she would accidently miss placing her cup in the holder and snatch up a green $25 chip from a neighbors stack. Placing the cup back in the holder she would let the coffee get too cold to drink. She'd then get up quickly to dump the cold coffee in a nearby trash can and pluck up the chip from the bottom of the cup before disposing of it. She never did it more than twice a night, but in a month she could average pilfering over $300 in chips.

This went on for an entire summer before security at one of the casinos finally caught up to her. One busy night Stephanie felt a tap on her shoulder while playing UTH. Tony sat at the next table playing Blackjack. When she turned around a rather large and intimidating man in a black suit asked to see her ID. She fumbled through her purse and showed it to him. "Ma'am, please take it out and hand it to me," the man said calmly.

Stephanie then noticed a second man, this one in a security uniform standing a few feet behind the black-suited man. Suddenly all eyes from the pit fixed on her. "Stephanie," the first man said politely, "walk with us, please, we'd like to ask you some questions."

Leaving her chips on the table she told Billy the dealer, who had a gob smacked expression frozen on his face, she'd be back in a few minutes. Stephanie nervously walked away from the tables escorted with the black-suited man walking a step in front of her and the uniformed security guard a step behind her. They led her into a small room near the east exit of the casino. The sign on the door said, 'Interview Room.' While all this happened, Tony covered his mouth with his hand, followed her with his eyes and shrugged his shoulders indicating "I have no idea" to everybody now turning toward him curiously with shocked expressions on their faces.

Another man dressed in a black suit sat at a large desk at the far end of the interview room. As Stephanie entered he gestured with an out-stretched arm for her to sit at a round table squeezed almost against the wall at the other end of the room. The two men who had escorted her stood rigidly against the far wall, one slightly to her left and the other slightly to her right. "Stephanie," the obviously higher in rank man at the desk calmly said to her, "Do you know why we've asked to talk with you?

"No sir."

"Well, Stephanie, you're one of our much-valued VIP guests. We appreciate that, but I just want to tell you about what the video cameras seem to have picked up."

As he said that he pointed to a camera in the corner above his desk. "By the way, this conversation is being seen and heard upstairs, just so you know."

"I figured as much." Stephanie tried to be as nonchalant as she could. She had instinctively placed her arms with hands crossed on the table top leaning forward to look as assertive as the interrogator.

Meanwhile back in the pit, Virginia the dealer at the Blackjack table who knew Stephanie and Tony very well stood shocked and repeated at him, "Tony, call her, will you call her. Find out what happened."

The other player at table, who also knew them, echoed the same concern. "Somebody must have done something to her. My lord, what's going on?"

Even the cocktail waitress working that side of the pit showed concern as she delivered drinks to the table. "Hey, you all," she said, "Stephanie can't be in any trouble." She put her hand on Tony's shoulder. "You're such nice folks. She must have reported something. Don't worry."

Ricky, the pit boss on duty, heard all this and came over to the table just as Tony started to get out of his seat. "Virginia, keep the games going. Tony I wouldn't go back there yet. I'll see if I can find out what's happening."

Ricky picked up the phone at the nearest pit kiosk and dialed security. About this time all eyes turned to the left as Stephanie, with the same two associates flanking her, arrived back at the tables. She stood with a grim look on her face, glanced at Tony and then let her gaze fall to the floor.

The black-suited associate instructed Jenny, the dealer who had replaced Billy, to color-up Stephanie's chips so she could cash them out. Jenny, obviously upset and concerned, nervously counted Stephanie's chips and colored her up with two $100 black chips, two $25 green chips, three $5 red chips, and four $1 white chips. "Two hundred sixty-nine, black out," Jenny said as red-faced as anyone had ever seen her.

"Go ahead," answered Ricky. He started to say something to Stephanie, but didn't.

With a confused look Jenny shakily pushed Stephanie's chips toward her. She also wanted to say something, but didn't. Stephanie, also shaking and not speaking, picked up her chips and gave Jenny a similar look.

The two security associates led Stephanie to the nearest cashier's window so she could cash out. They then escorted her through the casino to the east exit and to the parking lot. While all this transpired, she could feel every set of players' eyes staring at her. It gave her a combined feeling of extreme humiliation and distress. "Don't expect to see you here for 30 days," the black-suited associate politely reminded her as he opened her car door to help her in.

"Yes, sir."

Both security associates stood motionless as she backed out and nervously drove off the property. As soon as she stopped for a red light at the first intersection, she took out her phone and tapped Tony's name on her contact's list. When his phone rang, everything in the pit stopped for a second. Noticing this, he stepped away from the tables. He didn't answer until out of sight behind a row of Star Trek slot machines. "What the hell happened in there? Are you okay?"

"Oh ... my... God ... I was scared shitless."

"What did they do? What did they say?" Tony couldn't get the words out quickly enough.

"Just come home. I'll tell you all about it. I can't talk and drive at the same time right now."

Dennis and Betty, a married couple of casino regulars who had become friends with Stephanie and Tony, walked to him as he headed out. "I've got to go, Tony said. "I'll call you after I've talked with Steph."

Obviously concerned, Dennis put his hand on Tony's shoulder. "You let us know what's going on."

"Sure, I'll let you know all about it. Thanks guys." Tony answered as sincerely as he could muster. "Got to go now."

As he rushed toward the door Betty hollered to him, "Tell Steph we love her." Tony gave her the thumbs up without turning around. He then hastily disappeared out the door.

"What do you think she did?" Betty asked Dennis as they walked back to their table at the bar.
"I don't know," he scratched his head. "It could be she reported somebody doing something to her."

"Well, maybe so maybe not," Betty raised her eyebrows as they sat back down. "You just never know."

With that they ordered fresh drinks and continued watching the ball game playing on the TV monitor. "I wouldn't be surprised if Stephanie had taken to hooking." Betty offered the idea to Dennis as they drank what was easily a drink well beyond the point of no return for them.

Dennis already red-faced, glassy-eyed and slurring, grabbed Betty by the arm and told her in no uncertain terms that Stephanie and Tony were not that kind of people. He reminded her that Stephanie's paying for her sister's medical bills. "For heaven's sake, he's told us the whole story."

"I don't care. You just never know with these young couples nowadays."

"Doesn't mean anything." Dennis scolded her. "The booze is doing your talking now. It's not like she's wearing those god awful high heels and butt short skirts with her boobs all a twitching like some of them do."

"Yeah, like you'd do something other than look you drunk son of a bitch." Betty with her getting angrier by the drink tone of voice ended the conversation and got up. "I'm going to play poker."

"Go ahead." Dennis giggled. "Stay away from the guys with their 'coke spoons,' though, wouldn't want you getting poked by one of their long little finger nails."

"So what, security doesn't do anything about any of them milling around in here anyway."

It took Tony less than the usual 15 minutes to drive to the house. Luckily little traffic interfered with his speeding on the interstate. The fact that he hit every green light on the main street leading to their neighborhood helped, too. He rushed into the house and found Stephanie sitting on the bed smoking a cigarette, something she hadn't done in the house since taking her vow not to when they moved in. Deciding correctly to let that go for the moment he sat in the desk chair next to the bed. "Well, I guess that's that."

"No shit," Stephanie said sarcastically while blowing a puff of smoke into the air. "I've been banned for 30 days. They definitely know what I've been doing."

"Is that all they did, ban you for 30 days?"

"Yes, but they warned me in no uncertain terms that I better not do anything suspicious again."

"What will they do, take you in back and break your fingers?"

"Not funny, shit head, they don't do that kind of thing anymore."

"Did they say anything about me?" Tony asked nervously.

"No, but I bet your time is coming." Stephanie stubbed out her cigarette and immediately lit another. "I wouldn't try your little stunt anymore."

"Yeah, right, time for plan B. I'll get us a beer."

"As long as it's not hooking or drug dealing. I'm game for it."

"Life's a series of choices." Tony thought to himself as he headed to the kitchen. "We're getting in pretty deep."

5

Since Monday will be an at sea day cruising down the Gulf of Mexico toward Cozumel, where the ship will port Tuesday morning for the first of four shore excursion days, Stephanie and Tony spend most of the morning attending information sessions in the Starlight Theatre, soaking in some rays on deck 13 just above the pool area at the top of the ship, and reading. Tony plans on getting through at least 100 pages each day of *Insurgent* and maybe starting *Mockingjay*. Once they have enough sun, they head for the nearest air-conditioned area inside the ship. To their surprise, they stumble upon the library and an art gallery. "How wonderful," Stephanie says. "Let's check it out."

They admire all the artwork and then enter the library. Three other passengers sit quietly; an older man at a table reading a newspaper, and a mom with her young son at a bay window coloring. Tony notices three stacks of paper on a desk; one pile being a daily crossword puzzle, another pile being a daily Sudoku, and the other being a daily trivia quiz. "This is great, Steph, come look."

He snatches two of each and grabs two pencils sitting in a box on the desk. They sit down in a bay window and for half an hour work the puzzles and quizzes without saying a word. When they finish neither one realizes that the room had emptied. "Whoa, when did those other three people leave?"

"Beats me. Let's not forget to pick these up every day."

"Absolutely." Stephanie looks at her watch. "Hey, it's almost 2 o'clock. Let's go check out the shops on deck seven for a while."

Stephanie wants a hoodie. She heads straight for the women's clothing corner. Tony needs a new watch. He finds a table full of them. Before long Tony hears

Stephanie call him to come inspect a couple of hoodies she picked out. "I'm not buying today. They'll go on sale the last day of the cruise. I'll wait until then."

"And you know this because …"

"I know this because everyone I've talked to who has been on cruises before says so." Stephanie sneers. "Which one you like the light purple or the baby blue?"

"Don't care, Steph, either one's fine with me."

"I'll probably get the baby blue one if they still have it."

"Great, now help me pick out a watch. I need one with big numbers and a night light."

They search through the boxes until finding two possible choices that meet his criteria. "Which one you like the black one or the brown one? Tony says in his most sarcastic voice.

"Don't care, love, either one's fine with me." Stephanie sticks out her tongue.

He opts for the black one, mostly because it only cost $25, half as much as the brown one. As they continue browsing a familiar voice comes over the speakers. "Good afternoon ladies and gentlemen this is Caroline your Cruise Director with an important announcement. I'd like to introduce you to your Captain who has a few welcoming remarks for you."

"Bonjour, I am Captain Francois De Brea. On behalf of myself and the over 1,500 crew and staff members of the Swedish Gem, I welcome you aboard the finest ship in our fleet. We will dock in Cozumel tomorrow morning at 8 o'clock and leave precisely at 4 o'clock in the afternoon. Enjoy your day tomorrow. If you take a shore excursion don't forget to be back onboard by 3:30, s`il vous plait. Merci beaucoup, and bon après midi."

"Thank you, Captain De Brea," Caroline adds. "Let me remind everybody about tonight's show at 7:15 p.m. in the Starlight Theatre on Deck seven. It features our talented cast of international singers and dancers, The Troupe, who will take you on a nostalgic journey back to the 1970s and the days of disco in a show titled, *The Hustle*. See you then."

While listening to the announcements Tony notices a couple of unexpected faces sitting at a table in the lounge just outside the shops. A chill goes up his spine, tiny beads of sweat appear on his forehead, and he gets a sick feeling deep in the pit of his stomach. He grabs Stephanie's arm, and trying not to alarm her, quickens their pace down the corridor. As they reach the doorway, Tony glances backward. As he feared, the two men look right at them. When they raise their beer bottles in a mock toast, Tony knows the cruise has definitely changed course.

Dinner at Luxulos has a definite edge to it. Tony sits at the part of the table that allows him a clear view of the maître d's stand at the stairs by the entrance. He spends the entire meal distracted to the point where every time somebody descends the stairs to be seated his heart beats a little faster until he can identify that it isn't one of or both of those men he saw earlier. He has already scanned every table assuring himself that they aren't already in there. Stephanie, on the other hand, makes conversation that Tony barely hears. "How's your steak?"

"What? Oh, it's good, yes."

"Is something wrong?"

"No, the food's great." He gives her a fake smile while looking toward the entrance to check out the latest line of passengers waiting to be seated.

"That's not what I mean." Stephanie has a bit of an edge to her tone. "You seem distracted or something."

"Not at all. I can't wait for tonight's show."

Stephanie knows for sure now that something bothers Tony. He hates '70s music. She shrugs her shoulders and lets it go with, "Yeah, sure, rock on, dude."

The Starlight Theatre has three entrances; the balcony from deck eight, the lower level right from near the elevators, and the lower level left through the casino. That means Stephanie and Tony can play cards until almost show time. When they enter the casino after dinner, however, Tony's heart again skips a beat, blood drains from his face, and a wave of nausea overcomes him. There sit the two men at the UTH table. Tony mentally names them "Thug 1" and "Thug 2."

Stephanie knows quite well that she owes $15,000 to Snake, a loan shark back home who charges 10 percent interest. She also knows that she has a payment due the week after the cruise. What she doesn't know, because Tony hasn't told her, two debt collectors for Snake sit at the UTH table.

.

"Thug 1" has greasy salt and pepper hair. Cooter by name, he looks much older than his 45 years mostly because of the huge bags under his eyes, a result of a drinking two six packs of beer a night habit that started after his wife died five years earlier. Slender and tall, his eyes have a bit of a foggy look to them. He has a piercing stare with an eerie edge to his voice that makes people's skin crawl when he speaks, a perfect candidate to be a poster boy for the "kneecap crusher" cliché as debt collectors often got referred.

"Thug 2," a man named Hayes, looks much younger than his age of 42. About four inches shorter and 20 pounds heavier than Cooter, Hayes has unruly black hair with a permanent bed-head look. His voice, barely over a mumble, sounds like a morph of a foghorn and fingernails scratching a chalkboard. He also can chug beer one after another. They both look like they come from even deeper in the woods than Jimmy Brooks and his clan.

Nephews of Snake, Cooter and Hayes work for their uncle due to a promise "to look after them" Snake made to his younger brother Johnny while he serves his seven-year term in the Oklahoma state prison near McAlester for aggravated assault.

***

Stephanie first met Luther Earl Hackett a year ago when his wife and he came to a parent/teacher conference. She had their younger boy, Luther Earl Jr., in class. Young Luther, who looks just as rugged and unrefined as his father, was Stephanie's problem student. Luther Earl, known to everybody as Snake, owns a series of Laundromats in a 50-mile radius of area towns along the Oklahoma/Arkansas border. Moonlighting as a loan shark who plays in poker tournaments almost every weekend, he has developed a large cliental for his financial services.

Snake recognized Mrs. Shafer soon after the conversation about young Luther Earl's grades began.

Even though she had a different demeanor as Mrs. Shafer the teacher than as Stephanie the gambler, it didn't take long for him to place where he had seen her before. On occasion Stephanie and Tony play in a weekly "freeze out" Texas Hold 'em tournament at one of the area tribal casinos. Players pay a $60 entry fee and receive $4,000 in chips. Once play begins, they can buy an extra $1,000 chip for $5, but no other buy-ins beyond that. Once a player goes bust, they leave the table. Stephanie and Tony enjoy this format much better than regular cash games where players can keep buying in for as much as they want as many times as they want. The weekly tournament attracts 40 to 50 players with the winner's share usually over $1,000.

Twice Stephanie has played at the same table as Snake, once even knocking him out of the final table when her pocket queens beat his pocket jacks. Tony has also played at the same table as Snake a couple of times, but never at a final table. On one of those nights during a break, Stephanie overheard Snake discussing financial arrangements with another player as they sat smoking a cigarette and drinking a cup of coffee, something that could be managed during the 10-minute hiatus between rounds.

Snake weighs about 300 pounds, always wears a pair of overalls, and can stare a hole through a player. He always looks four days behind on shaving and changing shirts, but he does have a set of over-sized "bought and paid for" white teeth. He smells of Old Spice and Listerine.

***

When the formal conversation in Ms. Shafer's classroom ended, she exchanged handshakes with Mr. and Mrs. Hackett as she led them to the door encouraging them again to do a better job supporting their son's school work. Mrs. Hackett, obviously slightly perturbed by Mrs. Shafer's comment, abruptly excused herself with the standard "I need to visit the ladies room." At this point Stephanie casually mentioned that she recognized Snake from the Poker tables. He reciprocated and they idly chatted about cards for a moment. This gave Stephanie the opportunity to tell him a quick history of her mounting debt and her motives. He handed her his card, patted her on the back, and eagerly told her to call him if she ever needed his services. Two weeks later she did.

Stephanie borrowed $15,000 from him to replenish her checking account. Tony and she had agreed when they got married to have separate accounts. They divided up equally what each would pay for each month. They vowed not to question what either does with money left over after the bills get paid and groceries bought. They also promised to not carry any credit cards except for one to be used only for traveling or emergencies. So Stephanie had only one choice for a loan that she could keep secret from Tony – Snake.

She couldn't keep the secret for long, though. Her Catholic upbringing made the guilt of hiding something from Tony so great that she had to get it off her chest. One morning over breakfast after a rather intense session in bed followed by a joint shower she decided to disclose to him her secret. It didn't go over well, but Tony knew she had mounting losses along with her giving money to Rachel as often as she could. He didn't know the debt had reached $15,000. He couldn't complain too much either, he hadn't been on a winning streak for several months to the tune of $5,000, enough losses to end each month with barely enough balance in his checking account to keep it in the black.

As spring break and time for the cruise approached, they had their emergency credit card to rely on for travel expenses. "Good thing we've got plastic for the trip," Stephanie said as she dressed for school the Monday morning of the last week before spring break. "I'm a month late paying Snake."

"Good grief, Steph." Tony finished dressing for work. "Why didn't you tell me?"

"I talked with him. I told him I'd catch up after we got back. He's cool with it."

"Oh, and you know this because …" Tony came back with his familiar reply.

"Don't be silly, worry wart. We had a good laugh about it."

"What do you mean?" Tony's voice sounded a bit miffed.

"As I left his office he hugged me then shook his finger at me with that big toothy smile on his face." Stephanie imitated his scruffy voice. "You all have a good time.

Remember I know who you are and where you'll be." She then tilted her head back guffawing exactly like Snake.

Tony, however, wasn't convinced then it was a joke.

***

The color starts to come back to Tony's face, his heartbeat settles back to almost normal and he takes a deep breath to help relieve the nausea. He grabs Stephanie's arm. "Let's play slots."

He leads her down the aisle of slot machines out of sight from the tables. "I hear these Miss Kitty machines have been hitting pretty good."

"Okay, okay, okay," yelps Stephanie. "I'm game if you are."

They sit for 45 minutes playing Miss Kitty, Carnival of Mystery, Sirens, and Kitty Glitter penny machines until time to go to the show. Tony, playing max coins, hits bonuses on three machines ending up with over $300 profit. Stephanie, also playing max coins per spin on her machines, comes away just under $200 to the good. As they cash out and head to the theatre, Tony checks the pit. Cooter and Hayes still sit at the UTH table. He hopes they have no intention of watching the show and don't notice Stephanie and him hurriedly walking out of sight down the hallway to the lower level left entrance of the theatre.

They find two seats on the end of a row about halfway down the left center section just as the house lights fade. Showtime starts with a young wavy-haired Italian singer dressed in a white three-piece suit complete with flared slacks, a wide-collared brown shirt unbuttoned almost to his navel, and thick-healed gold-buckled shoes. Strutting out to the edge of the darkened stage with a spotlight following him he talks with a thick Brooklyn accent welcoming everyone to "da grand reopening of da most popular dance hall in 1970s Manhattan, Club Disco."

With that the lights come up on stage, *Night Fever* from *Saturday Night Fever* starts playing over the speakers, and the other five members of The Troupe appear in full disco garb singing and dancing to the magic of The Bee Gees and a strobe light.

Stephanie and most everyone aged 50 and older start moving to the beat. Tony, definitely not a fan of '70s music, sits with his mind on Cooter and Hayes. He figures if Snake has sent two of his hillbilly thugs to follow them on their cruise, something bad has to be in the works. With that possibility weighing heavily on his mind, Tony endures the show with his head spinning through a dozen or so scenarios of how to escape the watchful eyes of Snake's thugs without having Stephanie worry. Tony doesn't want her to catch on, at least not until absolutely necessary.

The show ends with a rollicking sing along of *Stayin' Alive* that puts the audience into a frenzied state of nostalgia. Even Tony politely joins in the standing ovation, though not nearly as engaged as Stephanie. When things settle down as the curtain finally closes and the house lights come up, Tony discreetly leads Stephanie to the far aisle that does not lead to the exit down the hall to the casino. "Hey, where are we going?" Stephanie's says still moving to the disco beat. "This isn't the way we came in."

"I know. Let's go sit at the bar and have a quiet drink."

"But the drinks are free in the casino." Stephanie breaks away from Tony and heads that way. "We can find a place in there. Come on."

Deciding not to give Stephanie any reason to question his behavior, Tony follows her in the casino. He orders two beers from the bar. He sees neither Cooter nor Hayes. Feeling a bit relieved for the moment, he motions for Stephanie to join him at the tables. She does. They spend the next three hours uneventfully playing UTH. By midnight, they have each drunk four beers and lost over $400. "Time to call it a night, Steph," Tony says yawning.

She takes one last gulp of beer, burps, and says both "excuse me" and "good night" to the other players. They walk back to their room. Stephanie swipes her card to unlock the door. Tony opens it for her. She walks in first. Her eyes catch sight of what waits on the foot of the bed for them. She jumps back and yells. "What the hell is that? Tony, what the hell is that?

"I don't know, Steph. It looks like a snake."

"A snake, how can there be a snake on the ship, in our room, on our bed."

"It's a towel animal, silly." Tony laughs.

"Oh my goodness, it is." Stephanie catches her breath. "It's cute, but it scared me at first."

"Duh, I know it did. I was here."

"Will we get one every night?"

Tony now in the bathroom brushing his teeth mumbles back. "I don't know. We'll have to wait and see."

Stephanie takes a picture of it with her phone. "It even has little beady eyes and a tongue." She names it Booger.

Tony rinses his mouth and heads for the toilet. Stephanie starts taking off her makeup. They change into sleep clothes settling into bed; Tony reading *Insurgent,* Stephanie reading the *Daily Cruising* brochure that gets delivered to cabins and staterooms each evening describing all the onboard activities and shore excursions available for the next day.

The ship will dock in Cozumel, Mexico, at 8 a.m. and sail at 4 p.m. "Let's check out the shops tomorrow," Stephanie suggests. "I've been told the t-shirts and other souvenirs sell the cheapest at this port."

Tony also has an idea. He tells Stephanie that some folks he talked to today said there's a secluded area of beach about two miles down the shore that not many passengers visit because it's not on the list of excursions. "We could have some real private time, if you know what I mean. We could buy some wine, hike on down, and maybe do it on the beach like in that old movie."

"Without the seaweed, I hope, but with plenty of waves." Stephanie had caught his references to both the famous beach scene between Burt Lancaster and Debra Kerr in *From Here to Eternity* and the parody of the scene in *Airplane.*

"And with plenty of sunscreen." Tony kisses her on the cheek and goes back to his book. Stephanie curls up next to him and playfully bites him on the arm.

6

"Good morning this is Caroline your Cruise Director." The announcement awakens both of them. "We'll begin going ashore in Cozumel in 30 minutes. Remember to carry your passport and be back aboard no later than 3:30 p.m. so the ship can sail at 4 p.m. Return to Pier nine, that's Pier nine. Enjoy your day in Mexico or onboard if you decide not to go ashore. We have plenty of fun activities planned."

Stephanie and Tony rush to get dressed, gather their gear for their day, and head out of the room by 7:55 a.m. "Got plenty of granola bars and bottled water, sweetheart?"

"Yes I do. We're out of here."

They get in line for the Deck four security exit and by 8:10 a.m. stand on Pier nine getting their bearings on what stands in front of them; downtown Cozumel in either direction flanked by shop after shop, restaurant and bar after restaurant and bar, and local police after local police. "Beautiful water, it's so blue," says Stephanie, "and so hot already. Let's head for the shops."

After taking a couple of quick photos standing in front of the 'Welcome to Cozumel' sign with the sea and ship in the background, they head across the walkaway to the first set of shops. For the next hour and a half American tourists Stephanie and Tony hear the same greetings over and over from attractive young Mexican men and women standing in front of every shop.

"Hola, amigos."

"Please come in, everything almost free."

"Free gift for you just to come in."

"Best souvenirs, best prices right in here."

They visit almost every shop and buy a couple of really nice $5 t-shirts. Most of the shops look the same carrying mostly the same items, but a couple of places do have a quirk that sets them apart. The last row of shops has a walkway with carvings of fish painted in various colors set in the concrete down the middle. At the last shop on the right an elderly shopkeeper stands with a bucket full of water. He throws out handfuls on the fish like seeding a lawn. "Sure is hot today. Got to keep the fish wet. Don't want them to dry out, he says. "Here fishy, fishy, fishy."

After having a good laugh at that, Stephanie and Tony turn to walk up the other side. In front of the last shop on that side another elderly shopkeeper stands in front of his establishment. He tugs at their arms motioning them to come in with him. "Amigos, since you walked far enough to come to the last shop, come inside and let me rip you off." He raises his arms in the air, smiles showing his yellow teeth, what ones he has, and takes a step toward Tony. "Hey, at least I'm being honest."

Amused by his candor, Stephanie and Tony go into his shop. Surprisingly, Stephanie finds a Mayan coin necklace she cannot live without. It's marked $50, but she offers the shopkeeper $35. Amazingly he counters with, "Because I like your purple hair so much, I give it to you for only 30 American dollars."

Stephanie jumps at that offer and says, "Deal."

Tony shakes his head thinking the necklace probably isn't worth more than $10. He doesn't say anything, though, and let's Stephanie have her fun.

Heading back toward the main street along the shoreline, Stephanie and Tony decide to stop in a bar to cool down. They order a Coke Light, what Diet Coke is called along the Yucatan Peninsula. While sitting inside at a table by the window front, they notice an elderly Mexican man hunched over a walker just coming into sight on the sidewalk by the far end of the 15-foot wide building. Not an inch over five-feet tall, he has dark, leathery skin. He wears an old straw hat. He has huge hands. He takes very slow steps. Tony points him out to Stephanie. "Look there's Slowpoke Rodriguez, Speedy Gonzalez's cousin."

They laugh. Continuing to rest in the air-conditioned bar while sharing the cold soft drink Tony imitates what Slowpoke Rodriguez often sings in the Speedy Gonzalez cartoons. "La…cu…ca…ra…cha, la…cu…ca…ra…cha." They laugh some more, but Stephanie scolds him. "You should be ashamed of yourself."

"I know. I am, but look at him."

Five minutes later they walk out of the bar refreshed. The little old man still has not traversed the 15 feet of the store front. What's more he's singing in a very low and slow voice. "ya…no…pue…de…ca…mi…nar," the second line of *The Mexican Cockroach Song.*

Ready to head to the secret beach, Stephanie and Tony start their 40-minute walk to what they hope will be a private and romantic day with plenty of time for some serious talk from Tony. He has a plan for losing Cooter and Hayes.

Admiring all the tropical foliage and wondering about who lives in all the shacks along their two-mile walk on the wide and open beach, they finally come to a grove of Royal Palm trees just past an abandoned lighthouse that narrows the shore to a sandy path. It hides them from the sight of the main road which runs about 15 feet above and 20 yards in from them. "Let's see if we can get in that old lighthouse," Stephanie says as she walks to its door.

It stands just four cracked concrete steps up from the beach. Its paint has faded from what once probably sparkled as a bright red to a dingy shade of pink. The glass windows at the top have cracked with one of the panes dangling.

"Be careful," Tony warns. "You don't know what kinds of critters might be in there."

"You're right." She steps back waving for him to go in first.

"No way, let's go."

Stephanie shakes her head defiantly and slowly pushes on the door. It opens slightly. She gives it a bigger push. As it opens all the way out runs a hairy tarantula the size of her hand. "Shit, let's get out of here."

"Someday you'll start listening to me." Tony yells as she runs from the tarantula and toward the path. It turns slightly inland and leads to the stretch of isolated beach surrounded almost in a half circle by the trees and various-colored foliage.

"Tony, this is fabulous. Water, sand, sun, and shade; it's perfect, hurry."

"Not bad, Steph, not bad at all," Tony comes around the corner, puts down his gear and plops on the sand for a siesta. Catching her breath for a moment Stephanie then throws off her flip flops, pulls off her t-shirt, nylon shorts, bikini top, and heads into the water. Tony manages to sit up long enough to watch before grabbing a granola bar and bottle of water from his backpack. "Looking good, girl, I like it."

"I certainly hope so." Stephanie waves and disappears into the cool, clean, clear-blue water. A few seconds later she jumps up shaking her hair and her boobs. Then she drops her purple bikini bottom that matches the purple streak in her hair and waves it in the air. "Break out the wine," she hollers.

Stephanie waves at a passing boat with two men aboard. One of them toots its horn and the other waves back obviously enjoying the far off view. Tony not amused yells, "Get out of the water and come over here now."

"Good grief, they can't see anything from that far away." Stephanie twirls her bikini bottom as she walks back to him.

"I don't care. Here, let's have some wine."

They drink half the bottle of wine before frolicking on the water's edge and again in the shade of the Palm trees. Satisfied and exhausted, they nap for over an hour. After awaking, they take a quick swim in the nude and then finish the other half of the bottle. Tony looks at his watch. He pleasantly discovers it to be almost 3:30 p.m. Needing to stay at least another 30 minutes so they will definitely miss the boat, just as he planned, Tony suggests they take one more swim before heading back.

Leisurely drying off, getting dressed, and packing their gear trying to take as much time as possible, he then leads her on a slow-placed walk back toward Pier nine. Checking his watch once again while she talks about their plans for the evening on the ship, Tony smiles slightly knowing it will have set sail before they arrive. Stephanie has no idea, much to Tony's delight. He knows, however, that things will get explosive in a few minutes. He works through several explanations in his head as he tries to keep up a conversation during the walk.

At 4:45 p.m. they get within sight of Pier nine. The moment of truth has arrived. In a few more steps he will be able to see if Swedish Gem still sits docked or if it has set sail. Tony's heart races as he spots a ship still in port. Taking a closer look, he realizes it is not the Gem at the end of the Pier nine walkway. It's the Royal, another SCA ship docked at Pier nine. Stephanie has not noticed yet, but she will soon enough. Tony has his story ready.

They begin to walk Pier nine. Stephanie suddenly stops. "Tony, where is our ship? That's not our ship."

"I know. You better sit down."

"That's not the Gem. It's the Royal. Where is the Gem?"

"It's already sailed. We missed it. It's 4:50 p.m.

"What? We were supposed to be back over an hour ago."

"I'm well aware of that."

"We missed our ship? Do you realize what this means? We missed our ship."

"I know, I know. Let me explain."

"Explain? You mean you know we missed our ship? You did this on purpose?

"Will you please sit down and listen to me. I can explain it all quite easily."

"You son of a bitch." Stephanie fumes. She sits down on a bench, crosses her arms and her legs, and turns away from Tony. "Explain away. This better be good."

"Remember the night at the casino back home when you felt somebody watching you."

"So what's your point?"

"Somebody was."

"What's that got to do with missing our damn ship?"

"I'm trying to tell you. Please, listen."

"Why should I. You've ruined everything."

"Somebody was watching you. I'm trying to save everything."

"Wait … What!"

"Somebody was watching you. In fact, it was two somebodies."

"I knew it. I just knew it." Stephanie turns back toward Tony.

"Yes, and those same two men followed us to New Orleans. They got on the ship with us."

"You mean the two guys in the old black car we saw at the gas stations? Are you serious? Who are they and why are they following us?" Stephanie's anger starts to subside.

"They belong to Snake. They're his thugs. You owe him a bunch of money."

Stephanie's demeanor instantly changes and color starts to leave her face. "Oh no … you're <u>not</u> kidding."

"No, I'm not and neither are they."

"Did they follow us today?" Stephanie's anger now has turned to solemn concern.

"No, they didn't. I'm sure of it. They're on the Gem headed to Belize and then Honduras."

"And we're not." Stephanie has an 'ah-ha' moment. "I get it. Nice plan. Why didn't you tell me?"

"I didn't want to worry you until absolutely necessary. Besides, I had to set things in motion first."

"Like what?" Stephanie now adds confusion to her demeanor.

"You know that Clark and Margie we talked with at the tables last night after the show?

"Yeah, the couple from Barling that drove the long way through Texarkana, Shreveport, and Baton Rouge."

"Well, those two thugs, Cooter and Hayes, played the tables, too. They heard us talking Clark and Margie into scheduling the same shore excursions as us for the rest of the week. I wanted them to think we would be off the ship on excursions every day."

"So they will schedule them, too, but leave us alone today." Stephanie catches on. Intrigue now describes her mood.

"Exactly. That's why I made a big deal about us not going anywhere but the crowded shop areas today."

"I get it, but what do we do now? We're stranded on Cozumel, a Mexican island in the Caribbean Sea off the eastern coast of the Yucatán Peninsula, for God's sake."

"No problem, we'll catch up with the Gem when it docks in Costa Maya Friday."

"And what do we do in the meantime?"

"Go to Costa Maya. Go snorkeling, visit some Mayan ruins, and do whatever else tourists do."

"And how do we get to Costa Maya from here?"

"Ride a bus, take a cab, or rent a car. It's less than 200 miles. We've got plenty of time."

"And what about clothes, hot shot? I'm not wearing the same clothes for four days."

"Of course not, dear. People don't run around Mexico naked, you know."

"Smart ass! What about food?"

"Look around. There are plenty of places everywhere to eat … whatever it is they eat down here. We'll be fine if we're careful."

"This is port. What about between here and Costa Maya?"

"We buy a cooler and carry goodies in them."

"Oh great, frozen chocolate cucaracha bars."

"It could be worse. You could be home grading those student essays on *"Why I'd like to be a bird."*

A moment later she wishes she was.

A crowd gathers at the dock. Residents and shop owners begin to shout, tourists wandering to their soon-to-be departing ship begin to move in, and police whistles begin to blow. Stephanie and Tony look just in time to see everybody pointing toward a tender boat coming into shore faster than usual and far off the marked course. It approaches and begins to slow. Tony grabs Stephanie's arm. "Oh, no. It can't be."

He pulls her away from the crowd. They start running in the direction of the beach where they had spent the afternoon, Stephanie stumbling to keep up. "It's them. It's Cooter and Hayes," Tony barks. "Hurry, we've got to get out of sight before they land and follow us."

They need to run for about 100 more yards of open shoreline to reach a small, tree-lined area where they can catch their breath for a couple of minutes and see, but not be seen. "I don't know what they had planned to do to us on the ship," Tony warns, "but on shore we might be in big trouble."

Meanwhile, Cooter and Hayes jump off the boat before the crew finishes tying it down. They had commandeered a passing tender boat from the Swedish Gem less than 30 minutes after it had set sail. They raced back to shore unconcerned about not only the dangerous, but illegal act they had committed. Describing Stephanie and Tony to everybody listening, they finally come across some people who point in the direction of where they have run.

***

Precisely at 4 p.m. as the Gem readied to set sail for its next destination of Belize City, Belize, a familiar announcement had begun. "Good afternoon ladies and gentlemen this is Caroline your Cruise Director with an important announcement. Passengers Stephanie and

Tony Shafer, if you're on board, please report to a member of your deck crew."

No word. Five minutes later the same announcement came again; still, no word. Another five minutes later the same message came again with the following added, "The ship will sail in five minutes if we do not hear from you immediately." Again, no word. Sure enough, five minutes later the ship set sail without Stephanie and Tony Shafer.

Cooter and Hayes, who had decided to confront Stephanie and Tony in Belize City the next day, then immediately put into action a spontaneous plan to hijack a nearby tender boat and head back to shore obviously "come Hell or high water." Their back woods instincts at that moment told them that the wrath of Snake would outweigh any consequences presented by the Swedish Gem personnel or local port authorities if they lost Stephanie and Tony so early in the week.

***

Stephanie and Tony see the two hugs running in their direction. Although a good 100 yards apart and temporarily out of sight, Stephanie and Tony think fast and act faster. "The abandoned lighthouse," Stephanie says. "Let's hide in there."

"Seriously, are you kidding? Who knows what else is crawling around inside. Not a good idea."

"That's exactly the point Tony, dear. Would you look in there if you didn't have to?"

"They're bound to look in it if they don't see us right away?

"So, we'll block the door shut so they can't get in."

With nothing else coming to mind, Tony shrugs his shoulders and gives Stephanie a little push in that direction. "Sounds like a plan, let's go for it."

Running along the tree line and stopping only long enough to catch their breath, it takes less than 20 minutes for them to reach the lighthouse. Cooter and Hayes are several hundred yards behind them. Stephanie and Tony take deep breaths, and nearly scared out of their wits, charge in. Barring the door shut with a couple of rotting wood planks they find on the floor they start a reluctant climb of a few steps. With only scattered rays of light and fresh air seeping through knot holes and the broken window at the top, the dark and dank structure stands wobbly as a temporary safe haven. At least that's what Stephanie and Tony hope as they stand quietly, aside from the occasional flicking off of real and imaginary critters of various shapes and sizes.

Tony peeks through a knot hole. "See them yet?" Stephanie whispers as she whisks a crawling something from the back of his neck.

"Hush, I can see them. We've got a couple of minutes before they reach us, though."

Cooter and Hayes approach. Stephanie takes a deep breath and squeezes Tony's arm. His heart races and beads of sweat form on his forehead. They both tense into statue-like stillness.

"Tony," Stephanie whines. "I'm scared shitless."

"Hush, here they come."

Stephanie closes her eyes and buries her head between Tony's shoulders. Tony grits his teeth and clenches his fists.

"Let's look in this old outhouse," Cooter says to Hayes.

"It's not an outhouse dumbass," scolds Hayes. "It's an abandoned lighthouse."

"Well, whatever it is. Let's give it a look see."

As they try to open the door a loud foghorn pierces the air from just off shore. Two members of the Gem's security staff, young men name Phillips and Merrill, along with a Cozumel Port Facility Security Officer Captain Gonzalez stand on the deck of a Coast Guard boat. "Turn around with your hands in the air," announces Gonzalez into his megaphone. "Are you carrying any weapons?"

Cooter starts to walk slowly toward the shore. "Freeze, senor," Gonzalez draws his pistol and aims it at them.

"We have no weapons, officer, sir," insists Hayes. "What's this all about?"

"Silence," barks Gonzalez looking quite intimidating with a large shiny gold badge pinned to the chest pocket of his black uniform. He nods toward Phillips and Merrill, who look less intimidating in their green and yellow uniforms with badges embroidered on their pockets. "I'm sending these amigos to bring you aboard. Do not move for you see I have a pistol aimed at you."

Hayes whispers to Cooter. "Let's make a run for it. What do you say?'

"No way, he's got a gun pointed at us and he's not more than 30 yards from us. Besides, those other two guys may be armed."

"Shoot, just because <u>we</u> can shoot a squirrel from 50 yards doesn't mean he can hit either of us from a rocking boat. Are you with me or not?"

Just as Hayes starts to turn to make a mad dash, two more black-uniformed clad officers approach jogging along the shoreline. "Never mind," he says with a sense of resignation. "Reinforcements have arrived."

Phillips and Merrill wade ashore and frisk both Cooter and Hayes. Phillips explains that Merrill and he come from the Gem. "You failed to follow protocol in disembarking the ship and boarding a tender boat. We are authorized by our ship's Captain to turn you over to the local authorities."

"We don't know what you're talking about, pal," Hayes says. "We're just tourists walking the beach. You've got the wrong guys."

Phillips and Merrill lead then toward the two local officers who have stopped less than 10 yards away with hands ready to draw their pistols. "Don't give them any reason to take out their guns," Merrill warns. "They'll shoot quick as look at ya'."

Stephanie and Tony remain tensely statuesque in the lighthouse to the point of breathing in unison and almost getting leg cramps from the tension. "You two can come out now," Gonzalez says, speaking with a much friendlier tone of voice and without his megaphone. "Hey, you two in the lighthouse, it's not safe in there. Come on out now."

Not sure what to do, but at last relaxing a bit, Stephanie and Tony take deep breaths and quietly move around trying to loosen their leg muscles. Phillips and Merrill shout to assure them that the two hombres are in hand and that it is safe for them to come out. "It is okay folks, we are not going to do anything bad to you."

Stephanie and Tony emerge from their hiding place. Squinting while their eyes adjust to the sunlight, they once again take deep breaths. This time not to release tension, but to take in the freshness of the ocean breeze. Gonzalez calmly asks, "You are Stephanie and Tony Shafer, are you not? Passengers on the Swedish Gem, are you not?

"Yes, yes we are," nods Tony. "We missed our ship. Time just got away from us today."

"Well, you need to come with me. I'm sure you're plenty stressed. I think you need some tequila, eh, and grilled Huachinango."

"Sounds good. That's an ocean fish, right?

"Si, senor, delicious fish. "You will love it en papillote with asparagus sauce.

7

Cooter and Hayes wade out and onto the boat accompanied by Phillips, Merrill, and their pistols. Gonzalez invites them to enjoy the below deck accommodations. Stephanie and Tony, meanwhile, board and stay above deck basking in the sun with Gonzalez as the boat heads back to port adjacent to downtown Cozumel. "How far is it to Costa Maya?" Tony asks Gonzalez. "We need to meet up with our cruise ship there Friday."

"It's about 200 miles of rough country, very dangerous for Americanos. You will not find the journey easy."

Stephanie cringes at that and gives Tony a hard pinch on the arm. "I no longer like your plan, hot shot. I don't like it at all."

"Let's have a nice dinner, Steph, not worry about anybody for now, and figure out what to do after talking with our new friend here, " Tony turns toward Gonzalez and the two make small talk so he can ignore Stephanie for a bit.

Below, Cooter and Hayes try to stare down Phillips and Merrill. It doesn't work. Finally Cooter breaks the ice. "So, we do get to go back to the ship with you guys, right?

"Yeah," adds Hayes, "After all, it's not like we're in custody or anything, right?"

Phillips points his pistol at them. "Not a chance you two. You've seen the last of the Swedish Gem for this trip."

"We'll catch up to the Gem in about 30 minutes," Merrill adds, "You, however, will by then be in a jail cell a lot smaller, hotter, and smellier than this."

The boat slows then stops with a slight thud and sways to the point of about knocking Hayes into Cooter's lap. All four of them have had enough of the combination fish, urine, and wet wood dankness of the below deck accommodations. As they climb out, Gonzalez shoves Cooter and Hayes toward two of his officers awaiting on the pier. "Take them to the jail. I will be there in two hours."

Phillips and Merrill assure Stephanie and Tony that they are safe with Gonzalez who comes across both formidable and jolly like the way a young Ernest Borgnine looked during many of his 1950s movie roles. His eyes glow bright and his smile mimics a Cheshire cat, but his husky build sends the message loud and clear that he can take on all comers. In an instant his eyes and smile, along with his voice, can change into the visage of an angry bull ready to charge.

Phillips and Merrill head down the pier to catch a waiting tendering boat that will whisk then to a rendezvous with the Gem that's on its way to its next port stop in Belize. Stephanie and Tony wish they could get back on the ship just as easily. "Can't we just go with you guys?" Stephanie asks.

"No, sorry," Phillips shakes his head. "It's against more regulations than you can count on one hand. I'm not even sure you will be able to re board in Costa Maya."

That catches Stephanie and Tony by surprise. "What does he mean by that?" Stephanie asks slightly bewildered and concerned.

"I don't know," Tony answers quickly. "He's probably just messing with us."

The two Swedish Gem security agents continue walking away and don't even acknowledge Gonzalez when he tells them "gracias y adios." They will file their report with the head of security on the cruise ship. He will then relay the information to Gonzalez giving him full authority to deal with Cooter and Hayes.

Stephanie and Tony look a bit worse for the wear as they step off the boat onto the pier. Stephanie turns to ask Gonzalez a question, but he puts his hand up and shakes his head, "I will answer all your questions at dinner, senora, just as you will answer all of mine. Let us now head that way. You have nothing to fear from me."

It's a pleasant walk to the Palmeras Restaurant in downtown Cozumel. Gonzalez uses the time to tell the story of the '"finest meeting place for Cozumelenos." It seems a young couple named Ruiz opened the restaurant in 1976 and it has since become an icon on the island.

Once they arrive at Palmeras, Stephanie and Tony head for the banos to freshen up. Gonzalez sits at his usual table. He waves off the server's attempt to hand him a menu and orders a bottle of tequila and fish fillet en papillote for three. By the time Stephanie and Tony join him at the table, three glasses full of tequila have been poured by the server who mixes a bowl of guacamole with a variety of spices for them tableside. He places a basket of multi-colored corn tortilla chips on the table along with the guacamole, a caddy holding four types of salsa, and the bottle of tequila.

Gonzalez makes a toast and gulps nearly half the glass of tequila while Stephanie and Tony sip. Gonzalez asks them why the two hombres follow them. He gulps the rest of his tequila and also asks why they purposely missed getting back on the cruise ship. Tony tells the tale. Gonzalez enjoys another glass of tequila and munches on the chips and dips with the gusto of a man who enjoys his meals.

Soon a banquet platter arrives along with three dinner plates. The platter contains heaping piles of rice and vegetables surrounding a nearly two-foot long grilled fish wrapped in a corn tortilla seasoned with asparagus sauce, onion, and cheese. The server opens the papillote releasing all the aromas of the entrée and then douses it with a generous pouring of white wine.

"You have many questions for me," Gonzalez says as he fills their plates with heaping helpings of the steaming fish, rice, and vegetables. "Let us eat and I shall answer them all."

"What's the best way to get to Costa Maya?" Tony asks.

"Your journey begins across the street," Gonzalez points with a piece of fish to the ferry terminal. "You take a 45-minute boat ride to the mainland."

The ferry runs every day, weather permitting, from 6 a.m. to 9 p.m., back and forth between the island and Playa del Carmen on the mainland of the Yucatan

Peninsula. The locals call the ride a "piece of cake," but more than few tourists find the ride a harrowing experience depending on the waves and the temperament of the crew. Two crews alternate days, and depending upon which crew, the ride is either an entertaining sing-a-long or a stomach-churning roller coaster-like ride. "Once on the mainland you choose riding the bus or renting a car."

"Which is better? Tony asks.

"Do you prefer the rice or the vegetables better with your fish?" Gonzalez answers with a question. "Both will get you there … eventually." Gonzalez leans back in his chair, wipes his mouth with a napkin, and builds a laugh that ends with another toast of tequila and a belch.

As they wait for coffee and dessert of crepes filled with caramelized milk served with vanilla ice cream and crushed walnuts, a house specialty, Gonzalez compares the two options. "The bus takes about six hours and makes at least eight stops. Sometimes the air conditioner works, and sometimes it doesn't. Sometimes the bus runs smoothly, and sometimes it doesn't. Sometimes the driver is sober, and sometimes he is not."

Tony and Stephanie do not like what they hear, but Gonzalez finishes with, "But everyone arrives safe and sound, always."

"So, what about renting a car?" Stephanie asks.

"A very good idea, usually." Gonzalez downs his third crepe, leans forward, and shakes his finger at the two of them. "Drivers in Mexico tend to be maniacs, particularly taxi drivers. Beware of taxis."

"Good advice." Tony looks at Stephanie. She gives him a nod of approval. "I think we'll rent a car. We've got four days and can do some sightseeing on the way."

"Good choice, very good choice," Gonzalez agrees, "but be careful."

Naomi and Jose, the couple that manages Palmeras, make their way over to the table and wave off the server as he tries to give the bill to Stephanie and Tony. "Dinner is on the house tonight for our new friends from America. We heard about your adventure today. Welcome to Cozumel Island."

Gonzalez gets up, gives a hug to Naomi and shakes Jose's hand. "You are too kind as always, you two." Stephanie and Tony join in the hand shaking and offer their appreciation for the fine meal. Tony gives $10 to the server. "I know what Captain Gonzalez means, now, when he says this is the finest place in all of Cozumel."

Gonzalez tells Naomi and Jose that their Americano amigos are going to ferry to the mainland then rent a car to Costa Maya. Jose warns them with a laugh. "Don't speed or do anything out of the ordinary or you run the risk of the dreaded encounter with the Policia Federal."

"Anything else we need to know? Tony asks.

"You drive on the right side of the road, however, the signs are in Spanish and left-handed turns are made from the right lane."

With that Stephanie and Tony say "gracias y adios" and head across the street just in time to catch the 7 p.m. ferry. After a short wait in the terminal as a boisterous crowd of both tourists and mainlanders form, they board to the sounds of old Beatles songs and the smells of a day full of passengers wearing too much sunscreen.

They decide to sit at the front of the boat so they can watch the sunset. They manage to find two seats in the fourth row.

To Stephanie's left come two middle-aged women. The breeze blows their cover ups just enough as they sit down to show everybody they're wearing bikinis neither of which flatter their fatter figures. Announcing that they live in Cedar Rapids, Iowa, and are "drunker that Cootie Brown," they pull their wide-brimmed straw hats down on their foreheads and start singing along to the Beatles song playing on the speaker, "Baby, you can drive my car."

To Tony's right sits a huge man with biceps as big as Tony's legs. He wears a Notre Dame cap backward on his head and sports intricate tattoos on his arms that look like something from Ray Bradbury's *The Illustrated Man.* He smiles at Tony which prompts him to ask the standard conversation opener, "Where you all from?"

"Arkansas now, but originally from Oklahoma. What about you?

"Evansville, Indiana, it's down in the southwest corner of the state."

"I've heard of that city," Tony replies. "We live in Fort Smith."

"Ah," acknowledges the huge man. "Whirlpool."

Whirlpool, the company that makes refrigerators and freezers for Sears, for many decades had plants in both Fort Smith and Evansville, as well as headquarters in Benton Harbor, Michigan.

"I'm Jimmy Pyle, nice to meet you."

"We're Stephanie and Tony Shafer, nice to meet you, too."

The boat captain welcomes everyone on board, does the obligatory safety lecture, and introduces the crew; Juan, Manny, and Roberto. After everybody puts on a lifejacket as instructed, it gets announced that in addition to Coke products rum punch will be served once the boat gets underway. Everybody cheers especially a freckled faced teenaged boy sitting across from and facing Stephanie. Upon hearing the announcement he grins, raises his eye brows, and belts out an extra "whoop."

He sits between his parents, his dad on his right with his mom on his left. "His mother and I agreed that he could have a glass of rum punch on the ferry tonight if he would go shopping with us today without complaining."

Getting approving nods from Stephanie and Tony, the boy introduces himself as Brent. "We're the Murphy's from Cleveland. It's our first cruise."

With the 45-minute ride well underway, the three crewmen start serving beverages. Juan passes around red Solo cups, Manny tosses cans of Coke products, and Roberto pours rum punch from a large plastic jug.

"Man, I'm thirsty," says Brent. He takes a big swig of his drink and lets out a pleasing, "Ah, that's what I'm talking about."

Dad laughs and clinks cups with his son. Mom frowns and sips slowly. After another round of rum punch gets served to anybody wanting a refill, which includes Brent, the Captain switches the music from old Beatles songs to the sounds of the Village People. Manny and Roberto, each buff, dark-skinned men in their mid-20s and full of energy, jog to the bow of the boat. They start dancing to *Macho Man.* A sing-along ensues. By the time *In the Navy* finishes Roberto has taken off his shirt, done a belly dance much to the delight of all the females on board, and started swirling a tie down rope over his head like a lasso.

More rum punch gets served and Brent's freckled face shines as red as a traffic light. "I think you've had enough, son," dad insists. "Don't you think so, too, Mom?"

"Aw, Dad, Mom, geez, I've been drunker that this lots of times."

Mom about has a cow. "Isn't it amazing what parents can find out about their kids once you get a little alcohol in them?"

Stephanie and Tony both laugh, but not too much. "Should be an interesting night in your hotel room."

By now the ferry boat draws within sight and sound of the mainland. A rousing rendition of *YMCA* blares from the passengers and crew. The lasso-twirling, belly-dancing, buff Roberto urges all to sing and dance louder so that "everybody in Playa del Carmen knows we're the best ferry boat crew on the Yucatan Peninsula."

As the boat docks a crowd gathers to cheer Roberto and urge him to do the full Monty. The passengers join in the chant. He starts to oblige, but the music suddenly stops. The Captain blows the horn. Roberto freezes. He raises his arms and yells on cue. "I guess not tonight, but maybe tomorrow."

Conga music plays and passengers prepare to disembark. Manny and Juan tend to the tie down duties. Roberto, meanwhile, showing his sweaty six-pack and his big smile, holds in one hand a white bucket with tips marked on the front with a black marker. With the other hand, he helps everybody step off safely. He receives plaudits, pats, and dollar bills from most everybody. He makes eye contact with each passenger and graciously says, "gracias y adios, amigo."

"Well, that was certainly interesting," Tony says to Stephanie as they step off the boat onto the pier.

She points to the left. "So is that."

About 20 feet away Brent, being held by his mom and dad, loses his rum punch and whatever he had for supper into a large trash can. When he emerges his red, freckled face has now turned a whiter shade of pale.

As recommended by Gonzalez, Stephanie and Tony stroll down Fifth Avenue and check into the quaint, inexpensive Hotel Casa Ticul for the night. They had an eventful day. They hope for a soothing bath, and a quiet, uneventful overnight rest.

8

Morning greets Stephanie and Tony with the sounds of children running the halls outside their door and taxis honking on the street outside their window. They can't believe it's time to get up already. "Wow," Tony says yawning and stretching. "I barely remember my head touching the pillow."

"I know what you mean," mumbles Stephanie.

Yesterday had been quite an adventure for them. Tony gets out of bed first. He makes his way to the window and opens the drapes. Not only the morning sunshine, but a majestic view of the turquoise water and white beach just across the street from them greets him.

Stephanie slowly emerges from her cocoon of sheet and blanket, shakes her hair, and stretches. Tony says, "Wow, quite a sight."

"Thank you," Stephanie squints in response to the sudden morning brightness.

"You, too, Steph, but I was referring to what's outside."

"Well, what's inside is pretty good, too, wouldn't you say!"

She joins him at the window pressing against his back side and giving him a warm hug. "It's lovely," she says. "It really is."

They take their time completing their morning ablutions. It's nearly an hour before they make their way downstairs for a breakfast of corn tortillas topped with eggs and a ranchero salsa full of onions, tomatoes and jalapenos. With two cups each of very strong coffee in their system, Stephanie and Tony finally head out into the morning sunshine for the walk up the busy street to the car rental.

A young boy about 10 years old stands just outside the door of the car rental. When he sees them cross the street and walk toward him he flashes a broad smile. "Buenos dias, you wish to rent auto?"

Before Stephanie and Tony can get inside the door, another youngster, this one a girl who looks just like the boy, flashes her smile and greets them with a rousing, "Hola, you rent auto from Papa?"

"Are you brother and sister?" Stephanie asks.

"Si, we are twins, Carlota y Carlos. We are 11 years old, but I am the oldest by eight minutes."

"Well, nice to meet you Carlota and Carlos. Yes, we would like to rent a car."

"Since you're the older," Tony adds, "do we do business with you or wait for your papa?"

Carlota laughs and promptly tells Carlos, the younger, to go tell Papa they have customers. "It is early and we just opened for the day. Papa is slow, but we are fast."

In less than five minutes Papa and Mama come in from the back. It's instantly obvious where Carlota and Carlos get their looks and demeanor. Mama sports a thin frame, thick hair, and a bright smile just like the twins. Papa, on the other hand, is as big around as he is short, has only a spackling of hair, and sports a nose on which one could hang a hat.

After seeing Papa's nose that rivals Cyrano De Bergerac's, Tony whispers into Stephanie's ear. "I wonder if there's a Mexican version of the name Roxanne." Stephanie punches Tony in the gut with her elbow.

"We need to rent a car to drive to Costa Maya."

"Bueno. My name is Santiago and this is my wife Rosario. You have already met our children Carlota and Carlos."

"We are Tony and Stephanie Shafer, nice to meet you. You have a beautiful wife and children."

"Muchas gracias."

"All we need is an inexpensive car for the day. I understand it's only about a four-hour drive."

"Si, for 25 American dollars I can put you in a new Chevy Spark. You like yellow or green?"

"We'll take the yellow," Stephanie quickly replies. "We're anxious to get on the road."

"Si, the paperwork will only take a few minutes. Rosario will bring the car to the back door and Carlota and Carlos will clean it for you, how you say, 'in a jiffy,' Si?"

Ten minutes later with great fanfare Stephanie and Tony head down Fifth Street and out of town to Hwy 307 South. Never before having had a sendoff from a car rental quite like they had just received from their new amigos Santiago and Rosario Alfaro, a word that ironically means lighthouse, and their children Carlota and Carlos.

"It's a wonder they didn't pack a lunch for us." Tony dodges a chuck hole and barely misses hitting a taxi coming the other way straddling the center line.

They plan on stopping just down the road in Akumal to buy enough clothes and supplies to last through Friday when they catch up with the Swedish Gem in Costa Maya. Extremely disappointed that they will miss the stops in Belize City, Belize, and Roatan Island, Honduras, as well as four days of free meals, free shows, and lots of casino time on the ship, Stephanie and Tony plan to make a few stops on the way to Costa Maya highlighted by visits to the Mayan ruins in both Tulum and Chacchoben.

The clothes they wore all day and evening yesterday and again this morning aren't too bad especially since Stephanie washed out their underwear in the hotel room sink last night, but fresh togs will be welcome. Stephanie tries to make a list of what all they need to buy in Akumal for the week, not an easy task while riding shotgun in a mini-car on the bumpy and narrow Mexican road. "Gee, I hope I can read this when we get there."

"No kidding. When I'm not dodging bumps and holes, I'll swerving to avoid crazy taxi drivers who don't seem to understand the concept of staying on their side of the road."

"Well, they've got to try and miss some of the bumps and holes, too, you know."

The little yellow Chevy Spark passes a police officer on a motorcycle just around the next curve. Stephanie smiles and waves to him. She doesn't give it a second thought when she looks in her side view mirror to see him edge onto the highway and follow them. When he turns on his red light attached to the handlebars and quickly catches up to them, she gives it a second thought. "Uh, oh, I think I just got us in trouble."

Tony looks in the rear view mirror. "Oh, shit, he's waving us to pull over."

"All I did was smile and wave at him. I do that all the time back home."

"Yeah, well we're not back home. Remember what they told us at the restaurant last night."

The officer parks his motorcycle in front of the car and walks to the driver's side. He has his hand on his gun and holster.

"Oh Lord, the Mexican Barney Fife," Stephanie whispers as she sinks down in her seat.

The officer struts from his motorcycle glaring at the car and them for a few seconds. He grabs the door handle on the driver's side. "Please step out of the car, both of you."

He leads them to the back of the car and pushes them just a tad harder than necessary against the trunk. "You are Americanos in a rental car driving too fast for this highway. I save you from maybe having a wreck."

Tony does not give the officer any resistance. He knows to stay calm and act polite. "Thank you, officer. We appreciate your warning. I'll be more careful."

Hoping to incite some anger from Tony, the officer tries another ploy. "Show me your driver's license and passport. Keep your mouth shut. I am not in the mood for your smart talk, hombre."

Tony gives Stephanie one of those 'we're about to really get in it now' looks. She starts to say something, but Tony shakes his head at her. The officer picks up on this. "Little lady, I need to see your passport, too."

"We don't have them on us, officer. We just have our driver's licenses." Stephanie manages to keep her cool and sound apologetic.

"You will follow me to Akumal, then. Your carelessness will cost you both quite a bit. Speeding is expensive enough, but now this."

Even though the officer stands barely five feet tall, he definitely has the 'little man syndrome' down pat; particularly his menacing tone of voice, piercing stare when he takes off his sunglasses, his invasion of personal space to establish his dominance, and his name tag "Tejada" being almost as big as his badge.

"Alright," Tony acknowledges. "I read you loud and clear. How much will it cost? We do not want to go to jail."

"A wise choice. I would say 50 American dollars from you and 25 more from the little lady ought to cover it."

"Fine, Officer Tejada, fine. We will gladly pay and be on our way, driving more carefully."

Tony stares at Stephanie and she gets his eye message to quietly get back in the car.

"That you will," warns Officer Tejada ensuring he gets in the last word. "I will follow you into Akumal to be sure you do."

When they turn off the highway and head toward the shore at Akumal, Stephanie and Tony are pleasantly surprised at the resort atmosphere. It's definitely another small, but beautiful tourist destination. With Officer Tejada finally turning off and heading to the small downtown area, Tony can now relax and freely find a parking spot where similar vehicles are gathered.

A warm breeze with the refreshing scent of the sea welcomes them. "Let's go buy some clothes." Stephanie grabs Tony's hand and leads him to the nearest row of shops.

"Sounds like winner." He smells his t-shirt. "That plus some other personal hygiene items as well."

Since Akumal stands for "place for turtles" most shops selling t-shirts have a distinct theme to them. In less than an hour and a half of visiting every souvenir shop Stephanie has a new backpack packed with four pair of denim shorts, two pairs of sandals, fresh underwear, a cosmetics bag packed to the hilt, a visor, and four t-shirts; pink, light blue, yellow, and tan – all with turtles on them.

Tony also has a new backpack packed not quite so full with four pairs of khaki shorts, fresh underwear, necessary personal hygiene products, and four t-shirts; navy blue, royal blue, brown, and Kelly green – of which only two have turtles on them.

They also buy a large cooler which they stuff with bottled water, bottles of Coke Light, granola bars, cheese crackers, chocolate bars, and apples. Using the restrooms in the lobby of the nearby Hacienda de la Tortuga & La Mirage, they freshen up and change clothes. Next stop the 700-year old Mayan ruins at Tulum, a drive of about 30 minutes that goes refreshingly uneventful.

Upon arrival Stephanie and Tony join in a group that has just gotten off a tour bus. They explore the site led by Balam, a muscular man who looks older than his announced 53 years. He claims to be of direct Mayan descent. As his first duty he introduces himself and explains that his name stands for the Mayan god of protection, a jaguar. He shows off his rather gaudy necklace with the likeness of a jaguar dangling from the chain. He advises everybody of the intense heat, the need to bring bottled water, and to spray for bugs. "The more you sweat, the more you get bit."

As the group hikes toward its first stop, Balam begins his lecture by telling the story that each Mayan city had a specific purpose and Tulum served as a trading seaport mainly dealing with turquoise and jade. "Tulum was the only Mayan city built on a coast, and as you can see, it was protected by a wall made of limestone."

During the walk to Castillo, a castle prominently perched on the edge of a cliff, Balam adds that historians and archeologists agree that about 600 people inhabited the city at its peak from the late 1300s through the early 1500s.

Ordinarily most of the castle stays off limits to tourists because of constant restoration activities, but this day careful climbing is allowed for a select few. "No children or elderly, please, just the young and strong," announces Balam.

Stephanie looks at the steep steps leading to the top of the castle and decides not to trek up them. Tony insists she try because the view is supposed to be spectacular. "Come on, Steph, you can make it."

"Bite me."

"Suit yourself, sissy britches."

Stephanie takes a slug from a cold bottle of water and decides to 'man up' and climb. Once they arrive at the top, a feat not everyone in the chosen group of "the young and strong" accomplishes, Stephanie looks at the amazing view and admits to herself, but not Tony, that she's glad she made the climb. She also very much appreciates the cool breeze coming from the sea.

Balam lets the successful climbers catch their breath, enjoy the view, take pictures, and make their way down before continuing his talk. "As you can see, invaders could be seen well in advance. Peasants protected the priests and nobility, a major reason why my people lasted so long."

In front of Castillo majestically sits Temple of the Frescoes, which appears well preserved and in which tourists can enter. Balam invites them in. "Peer inside to see the mural painted in three sections, but drink some water before entering. It is very hot inside."

Tugging at sweaty shirts and swatting away bugs, the group of 17 tourists made up of six men, six women, and two teenaged boys almost simultaneously look at each other and reluctantly head into what they now know will be an even hotter place than where they stand in the blazing sunshine. "Oh my," says an older women fanning herself with her hat, "we're going from the frying pan into the fire."

Once everybody crowds into the temple Balam explains what they see. "The first level represents the Mayan world of the dead, the middle level is that of the living, and the highest level is the creator and rain gods."

One of the teenagers in the group notices something on the middle level. "Is that a horse?"

"Interesting that you think so, young man," Balam replies with an impressed tone to his voice. "If that animal is a horse, then that means Mayans still lived here in 1518 when the Spanish first arrived."

"I don't get it," the teenager adds. "There weren't horses here already?"

"Oh no, the Spanish brought the first animals here in 1518."

Exiting the crowded and hot chamber along with everybody else, Tony notices a figure chiseled above the doorway that looks like a bird's wings and tail. "I keep seeing this same image on a lot of the buildings."

"Yes, indeed," Balam nods. "It is believed to represent a Mayan deity swooping down to protect the people." He takes off his hat and wipes his brow. He suggests everybody take another breather. "Not a lot of shade, have you noticed?"

The older woman once again fans herself with her hat as she sits down on a concrete ledge. "I think I know what happened to these Mayans, they melted."

"Yeah," agrees a man sitting next to her. "No bottled water in those days." He takes off his bucket hat and pours some of his bottled water on his bald head.

Everybody laughs. Stephanie pokes Tony on the arm. "Aren't they a sweet couple? That's us in 30 years."

Just past Castillo a pathway leads down to the beach. "Free time the next 30 minutes for you to enjoy the beach, roam around the ruins on your own, or visit the market," announces Carlos. "I will stay here to answer any questions."

Stephanie and Tony decide to join the few others who walk down the path carved into, around, and under nooks and crannies in the cliffs. Once they arrive at the beach they decide to take a swim in the Caribbean. Since they have swimming togs on underneath, they casually chunk off their sandals, drop their shorts, and pull off their shirts. Not in any hurry since not part of the tour, they stay in the water until everybody else heads up.

Once onshore they share a package of cheese crackers and a bottle of Coke Light Stephanie packed in her purse. They then take a walk before heading back up and out to their rental car.

Drenched in sweat, they freshen up in the restrooms adjacent to the market. They poke around looking at souvenirs for a few minutes. Stephanie buys a refrigerator magnet and a shot glass. She tries to talk Tony into buying her a floppy straw hat, but he declines rolling his eyes and huffing. "Can we please go now?"

Once on the road, Stephanie out of the blue blurts, "I wonder what will happen to Cooter and Hayes back in Cozumel?"

"What makes you think of them?

"Oh, I don't know. I guess the prospect of us maybe going to jail in Akumal."

"I'm sure Captain Gonzalez will talk them to death," Tony once again avoids both a chuck hole and a small tree branch on the highway.

Stephanie buckles her seat belt. "Maybe he could have them fill in all these holes in the road. That will keep them busy for a while."

"Well, no matter what happens to them, you still owe Snake $15,000."

"Thanks for the reminder, asshole. I really needed to hear that right now."

"Sorry, but it's a real problem and it isn't going to just go away."

"Can we talk about something else?"

"Sure, but you're the one who brought it up."

"Let's not talk at all." Stephanie turns away from Tony and stares out the window. Her thoughts focus first on the money she owes Snake, turn to Rachel's pregnancy issues and struggling marriage, then to her worries about the stress to her parents, and finally end up on the fact that she is ovulating this week.

Tony starts to quietly sing *YMCA*. Stephanie cannot hear him over the droning of the air conditioner on full blast trying to keep the car cool as it buzzes south on Highway 307 toward Felipe Carrillo Puerto, about an hour away.

Skinny cows grazing on nearly grassless pastures, acres of sparse droopy crops, and occasional people sitting about fruit stands cluttered with homemade novelty items for sale dot the drive toward what was once known as Chan Santa Cruz, but now named for a former 1920s governor of Yucatan, Felipe Carrillo.

Finally breaking the silence after about 20 minutes Tony looks at Stephanie and states the obvious, "Not much to see on either side of the road."

"You can say that again." Stephanie straightens up and sighs. "I'm getting hungry."

"We can stop in that Felipe whatever place. We'll be there in about half an hour."

Sure enough in about 30 minutes they hit the outskirts of Felipe Carrillo Puerto. Unfortunately, about a minute later they find themselves on the outskirts of the other end of town.

"Uh, is that it? Tony, is that it?

"Never been here before, Steph. But yes, I think we just saw it all."

"A gas station, a bank, a clock tower, two hotels, a church, and a plaza; did I miss anything?

"I don't know, let's turn around and take another look."

"I'm hungry and need to pee," Stephanie repeats with a bit more urgency than before.

"Well, it looks like that's the nicest place in town," Tony points to Hotel El Faison y El Venado. "Are you game?

"I said I'm hungry and need to pee. Let's check it out."

They enter a reasonably busy restaurant full of locals and instantly notice the familiar aromas of Mexican spices and sauces. Impressed they find a table near the restrooms. Tony sits and Stephanie heads for the banos.

The restaurant looks better and more upscale than the hotel lobby, and Tony takes in the sights and sounds waiting for Stephanie. When she comes out, he takes his turn.

A waitress drops off two menus and welcomes them with a greeting that results in a round of laughter from the locals. "Hola, amigos, you do not have to remove your shoes or hats in here."

Feeling a bit puzzled, Stephanie and Tony don't quite know how to react to that and all the commotion. "While I get your drinks, Niguel will tell you what I mean."

"Do not be offended, my friends, we are happy to have you dine with us. I am Niguel, the hotel manager and I will tell you about our humble village."

"Nice to meet you, sir," Tony stands and shakes hands with Niguel. "I am Tony Shafer and this is my wife, Stephanie. We are driving from Cozumel to Costa Maya today."

"Lovely, quite lovely to meet you both," Niguel replies. "Please, sit down."

"First, let me recommend the house specialty for your meal," Niguel grabs the menu from Tony. You must try the grilled venado steak."

"Really. Tell me more."

"It is deer steak paired with pickled red onions and habanero chile sauce, very fiery and feisty."

"Really, deer meat, you say."

"I'm more in the mood for chicken," Stephanie quickly adds trying to save the moment.

"Ah, then you must have the chicken pibil." Niguel approves, "It is also very spicy and very good."

Niguel waves toward the waitress, "Elena, two servings of chicken pibil for this table, heavy on the sauce."

"Would you care for a bottle of red or white wine?" Elena asks.

"Actually, how about a couple bottles of Coke Light?'

"Oh, I am so sorry, too early in the afternoon for you to drink wine," Elena replies.

"No, no, not that, I still have a bit of a drive to Costa Maya and we'd really just like a soft drink."

At this point Niguel begins to explain the joke from earlier. Apparently, the only attraction in Felipe Carrillo Puerto consists of a shrine dedicated to the talking cross, a symbol of the Maya people's struggle against inequality and injustice. Housed in a thatch-roof sanctuary next to a dried-up cenote (natural sinkholes that form when the roof of a cavern collapses) in a small park about five blocks south of the town's only gas station, no one may enter the sacred shrine wearing hats and shoes.

Stephanie and Tony have a good laugh, much to the delight of the locals, and anxiously await for their food to arrive so they can eat and make a quick, but polite exit. Munching on platano chips and a curiously sweet dip, they try not to sweat. The light breezes coming through the windows and the ceiling fans with only two blades rotating at about one revolution per minute cannot compete with the steaming heat coming from the kitchen and the near 100 degree temperature of the outside.

The chicken pibil entrees arrive and bring to the table a pleasant aroma, particularly the sauce. Stephanie takes the first bite and proclaims the chicken as excellent. Tony takes his first bite and agrees. "Hey, this is great."

"Really hits the spot," Stephanie says. "I love the sauce." In less than ten minutes they have both cleaned their plates and finished their Cokes. Knowing that a request for dessert will soon come from Elena, they hurriedly leave the table and head for the register.

Before Elena can make the offer, Tony has taken out his credit card to cover the $17.38 bill insisting that they are stuffed and really need to get back on the road.

"Oh, so sorry, folks, we take cash only, no credit cards."

Not what Tony wants to hear since they have already been inappropriately relieved of $75 back near Akumal.

He digs into his wallet and reluctantly pulls out a $20. "No problem. Please, keep the change."

With full bellies and a shrinking supply of cash, they exit through the hotel lobby and cram again into the little car. "Onward to Chacchoben and more ruins to see."

"I'm with you all the way, love. Let's go climb another pyramid."

Forty-five minutes later at the turnoff to the west that leads to the ruins site, the car almost bites the dust. A tour bus, which Stephanie and Tony caught up to about five miles back, suddenly veers to the right and comes to a stop with its front half fully off the highway and its back half jutting about two feet into the highway. Because of a small ditch, it's leaning a little to the right.

To avoid ramming into the back end of the bus Tony slows down the car and crosses the center line. He intends to make the right hand turn at the intersection and pull off on the flatter shoulder of the road leading to the ruins. As Tony makes this adjustment the driver suddenly appears from around the front of the bus almost running into the car. Since the tour bus has only a passenger side door, Tony could not notice that the driver had gotten off. Stephanie screams and Tony lurches the car to the left ending up in a shallow ditch on the left side of the road stopping just about six inches from a fence post with barbed wire dangling from it.

Taking a moment to collect themselves before getting out of the car, Stephanie hollers, "There's a dog in the middle of the road, and it's been hurt."

The bus driver carefully approaches the distressed dog. He stretches his arms out to signal for everybody to keep away. He looks at Stephanie and Tony to see if they are OK. Tony slowly approaches announcing that he and Stephanie are fine. The bus driver nods his head and again signals them to keep back.

"What happened, did you see?" asks Tony.

"It's been in a fight," the bus driver says. "Look at all those bite wounds."

Stephanie walks around the back of the bus and on up to the passenger's side door. A few passengers get off while others gaze out the left side windows. "Be careful, a dog has been in a fight and is badly hurt. Stay back."

The dog, a mangy looking female Bull Terrier with a single brown spot on its face, struggles to get up. Her left ear appears half bitten off, her left front paw bloody, and there's a gash on her left hind quarters exposing some bone from where her skin has been ripped away by a vicious bite. She howls in pain, starts drooling and falls in a heap.

"We need to take her out of her misery," the bus driver says quite emphatically. "Come look. She is too bad off to help, don't you agree, senor?"

"You're probably right." Tony nods as he carefully squats down to get a closer look. "But what can we do?"

"Get everybody back on the bus and in their seats, please."

While Tony and Stephanie tend to the bus driver's request, the driver cautiously approaches the dog. He squats and slowly shows his hand to her. She does not resist. He pets her back feeling for other injuries. He lifts her head and winces when he discovers a bloody gash on her neck. Taking a deep breath he whispers "easy girl, easy now," and quickly snaps her neck. He stands up, takes off his vest, and gently places it on her head.

"Senor," he hollers to Tony. "The deed is done. Now we must move her to the ditch."

A passenger hands Stephanie a bottle of water and she pours some on the blood stains in the road. She also pours some on Tony and the driver's hands. She digs out some napkins and a small bottle of hand sanitizer from her cosmetics bag in the car and pours a generous amount on their hands, as well. Trying not to cry, she consoles the bus driver saying, "You did what you had to do. She's no longer suffering."

"Gracias," he replies sadly. "The wounds were fresh, this must have just happened. I see no other animal, though."

"What do you think got her?"

"Many young men in these parts have pit bulls," the bus driver admits with a bit of disgust to his tone of voice. "They raise them to be wild and aggressive."

Quietly, he returns to the bus as do Stephanie and Tony to their car. They back it out of the ditch and wait for the bus to take off. The bus driver waves as do some of the passengers. The vehicles turn to the right and head toward Chacchoben, the bus containing tourists considerably more somber than before.

"Please let there be lots of trees," Stephanie pleads as they approach the entrance to the ruins site. "I can't take another hour of no shade like at Tulum."

"It wasn't that hot, now really."

"Oh yes it was."

Stephanie and Tony once again join with the bus tour. This time, however, trees line the path into the ruins. Waiting for them under a shady tree about 50 feet down the path stands the tour guide. "Welcome to Chacchoben, the place of the red corn. I am Acan, your tour guide. I am of Mayan descent named for a spirited, fun-loving Mayan God most famous for enjoying adult beverages."

"Cheers," hollers one of the tourists as he raises his bottle of water. This brings a round of chuckles from the tour members.

"Ah, a spirited, fun-loving, group," Acan responds with a hardy laugh. "My namesake would approve."

Before beginning the hike through the sparse forest containing the ruins, Acan begins his talk with the inevitable reference to the supposed planet-wide cataclysm that was to occur in 2012.

"Doomsday, the apocalypse, the end of time. According to many interpretations of the Mayan calendar, December 21, 2012 was to be the end of humanity. The sun was predicted to shift causing violent earthquakes globally. The calendar would reset to zero and the Mayan Gods would return to restart civilization." Acan tells the story like an accomplished orator performing for an audience.

"We of Mayan descent knew better. We saw the end of 2012 as the beginning of a new age of hope. A time when all humanity would finally look beyond their differences and begin to value their similarities."

The group heads toward the first restored temple. Acan continues his history lesson. "The Mayan civilization here peaked for about 600 years into the 10th century. They contributed greatly to our modern-day understanding of astronomy and mathematics."

About this time the group reaches a massive temple that Acan says dates back to about 700 AD. It has been recently restored using the same materials as the original. "As you will see, not all the original structures have been restored yet, but eventually they will be."

Acan explains that the Mexican government didn't know about the ruins until 1972 when an American archaeologist stumbled upon the site while flying a helicopter during a project for a Canadian museum. "He noticed numerous hills in these flat lands while helping local farmers locate rubber trees. On closer look he realized they were temples naturally covered over a period of many centuries."

Members of the group climb partway up the temple to a roped-off area that is still being restored. It's a chamber that Acan claims may have been a meeting place for the nobles. "This temple's restoration began in 1994 and opened to visitors in 2002. It is expected to be completed by next year."

After picture taking with most tourists clicking cell phones and only a few using actual cameras, the group follows a circular path that includes more pyramids in different stages of restoration as well as the remnants of the common area that served as the main gathering place. Some of the structures still have traces of the red paint with which they were originally coated that are evident because of the many trees shading their exposure to the sun.

The village contains many species of fauna including fig, banyan, mahogany and palm trees. Lots of birds and spider monkeys inhabit the area as do deer and fox. "Deeper in the surrounding jungle roam jaguars, pumas, ocelots, and tapirs," Acan cautions. "They do not come near the ruins, though."

Soon the group comes upon the main attraction, a six-story pyramid high on a hill that requires a climb of 50 steep steps to get to. About half the group, mostly the men, attempt the climb. Tony leads the pack, and on arriving first at the top after a brief rest period about halfway up, serves as cheerleader urging the others to finish the climb. "Just a few more steps, you can make it."

In front of them stands the foreboding restored structure. "Who's going to climb with me to the top of it?" Tony boastfully asks.

"Let's not, and say we did," quickly answers the last man to make it to the top of the steps. He plops down on the ground almost out of breath.

Off to the left, the men, most of whom huffing and puffing and wiping sweat from their heads, see the women approaching. They walk a considerably less severe winding path to a plateau only five steps below and about 50 feet from the base level of the pyramid.

"Hi guys," mocks Stephanie. "What's up?"

"How did you all get up here?"

"If you hadn't been in such a hurry to do the macho man thing you would have heard Acan tell us about the easy way up."

"Oh."

"Yeah, try listening next time."

Tony heads for the pyramid and begins his ascent. He stops about 15 steep steps up and stands in a crevice. "Come on up, Steph," he yells as he waves at her. "Here's a good place for a photo."

"Fine," she huffs. "Don't expect me to climb any higher."

Stephanie hands her cell phone to one of the women who volunteers to take the picture. She easily navigates the 15 steps and joins Tony in the crevice. The others watch and when Stephanie comes down she volunteers to take pictures of whoever else wants to pose in the spot.

While that's going on, Tony continues his climb determined to make it all the way to the top. No one else follows. Three rest periods later, drenched in sweat, and having drunk an entire bottle of water, Tony stands at the peak doing the arm-raised Rocky Balboa thing. He waves to the applauding gathering below and poses for pictures being snapped by a bevy of cell phones.

Tony, however, on the way up never thought about the way down. As steep as the steps are going up, they are just as steep going down. With no handrails to use for balance, he decides the only way to make it down safely is to side step in a zig zag pattern. Trying to look cool and unconcerned he begins his descent. "Shit," he says under his breath, "what a stupid idea this is."

Resisting the urges to lean too far forward or go too fast, Tony slowly makes his way down. He waves with a smile about every 10 steps and stops for a rest period only twice. Finally he reaches that crevice only 15 steps from the base. "Anyone want a picture with me?" he asks amusingly, using that as an excuse to catch his breath from the effects of the heat and humidity.

To his surprise three women actually do. After the photos, Tony offers to walk them down and holds their arms as they reach out to him for support. Stephanie greets him with a sarcastic "what a guy," and puts her arm around him. She smiles to the group. "My hero."

He knows, however, what she's really thinking. "Dumbass," she whispers in his ear. "That was the stupidest thing you've ever done."

"I could use a cool down," he boastfully says to the group. "Let's head to the gift shop and snack bar."

Acan points to the easy way down, "This way, folks, only one more stop before we return to the entrance."

Returning to the common area, Acan stops at a chicle tree. "When you chew gum, you're more interested in its taste than with its history. But if you ever wondered about the origins of your gum, it comes from the sap of this type of rubber tree."

He tells the story. "In 1869 the famous Mexican General Santa Anna (Remember the Alamo!), thought he could commercially exploit the properties of chicle. Unaware of its chewable virtues, he hoped chicle could be exported as a rubber substitute. He passed it along to an American inventor Thomas Adams who found chicle unsuitable as a base for rubber. Intrigued by the texture of chicle after it gets boiled, he decided to roll some in sugar. He chewed some and it lasted far longer than any gum available at the time. Quickly his boiled chicle vastly outsold all other varieties of gum and revolutionized the industry."

Acan pulls a package of Chicklets out of his pocket, "Now you know where this gets its name."

"How cool is that!"

"Wow, I didn't know that!"

"That's really neat!"

Enjoying the usual responses to his 'grand finale,' he raises his arms and then points to the path leading back to the main entrance and announces the tours end. "If you have questions, I will answer them as we walk to the air conditioning waiting for us in tourist center."

Parched, Tony buys an ice cream bar and quickly sits at the nearest table. Stephanie heads for the gift shop. She eyes the floppy straw hat shelf and smiles. She takes off her sweaty visor and heads to the ladies room to rinse off the sweat and fix her hair as best she can. With no intention this time of asking Tony to buy her a floppy hat, she tries on several. Finding the one she likes best, she keeps it on and walks over to peruse the t-shirts. She finds a yellow one that matches the color of the scarf tied around the brim of her new hat.

She picks out another refrigerator magnet and shot glass to add to her collection. Meanwhile, Tony downs a second ice cream bar and heads for the gift shop to kill some time and stay in the air conditioning. He sees Stephanie in her new hat. He can't resist admitting to her just how cute it looks, especially when she flashes her 'I told you so' smile at him.

"Look what else I got." She pulls out the t-shirt. "See, they match."

"Very cute, dear."

"Want one? I think it will be precious for us to have matching t-shirts."

"Uh, no, I don't think so. I'm not into precious."

"OK, then, how about a different colored one, as long as it's not blue."

"Fine." Tony gives in. "Pick out one, I don't care. Surprise me."

She finds a masculine looking one in a medium brown with just the words Chacchoben Mayan Ruins written on the front in burnt orange.

They make their way to the car and drive back to the intersection of Highway 307. Before turning right to head to the turnoff that takes them the final hour of the drive to Costa Maya, they pause and look at the almost washed away blood stains of the dead dog who still lays in the ditch with the driver's vest covering it.

"Poor baby," says Stephanie. "I hope someone picks her up before birds get at her."

After a few miles down the highway, they turn left onto the road to Costa Maya. They quickly discover that as bad as the highway is, this road is even worse. The car bumps and grinds along the road that has as much dirt and rock as it does asphalt. "I feel like we're riding an old, narrow wooden rollercoaster. I almost have to get off the road anytime a bus comes the other way."

"Quite a day," says Stephanie. "And I thought yesterday was something."

"Who knows what tomorrow will bring," Tony whispers in a sinister tone of voice like the announcer from the old radio show *The Shadow*.

"Not funny."

9

Upon arriving in Costa Maya after bouncing around the last hour in the car, Stephanie and Tony choose the Hotel Costa Maya Inn on the far end of the boardwalk in an area called Nuevo Mahahual. It's only 10 minutes from the port where all the cruise ships dock. The three-story hotel stands peacefully and quietly with vacant lots on either side and across the boulevard. It has a large pool in back with several cabanas surrounding it. A hot tub sits on the far end.

Looking a bit ruffled and tired, they enter the lobby with their backpacks and cooler in tow. Evelin, the self-proclaimed 'hotel clerk extraordinaire,' greets them with huge smile. "You look like you two could use something cool."

She directs them to sit at a bamboo settee in the middle of the lobby. "Best pineapple juice you will ever drink," she boasts as she pours each of them a full glass. "We have the sweetest ones along the Yucatan Peninsula."

They both sit back, put their feet on the bamboo cocktail table, and take a couple of hardy slurps from the straws with little red umbrellas attached. "Boy," that really hits the spot." Tony clinks glasses with Stephanie.

"Live long and prosper." She gives the Vulcan salute.

"Warp factor five."

Evelin looks at them with a furrowed brow. In a few seconds, though, she catches the reference. "Oh, outer space show. I see that on my TV."

"We need a room until Friday, if we may," Tony requests.

"You do take credit cards?" Stephanie quickly adds.

"Why sure I do. I have plenty of rooms now that the weekend is over."

"Sounds good." Tony finishes his pineapple juice and heads for the registration counter.

Stephanie takes her drink with her and heads for the glass doors leading to the pool. "May we have a room close to the pool? It looks beautiful."

"You will enjoy it, no doubt," Evelin brags, "a great place to relax."

The paperwork finished, Stephanie and Tony head three doors down the hall to their room. Once in, they toss their backpacks on the floor, set the cooler down, and plop themselves down on the queen-size bed. "Ah," Stephanie sighs, "much better than the car."

"And almost as big."

A few minutes later they get up to put their clothes in the generous drawer space available on the dresser against the wall. Stephanie takes the top drawer and Tony takes the one under it. A 32-inch LCD TV sits on top of the dresser. Next to the drawers a cabinet door hides a small safe and small refrigerator.

Stephanie opens the drapes to reveal a beautiful view of the pool. To her surprise, the window she expects to see is really glass doors. "How nice, we can get straight to the pool from our room."

"What are you waiting for?" Tony emerges from the bathroom with his swimming togs on and a towel wrapped around his neck. "Last one in is a rotten egg."

Stephanie pushes him on the bed. "No fair. You wait for me."

He checks out the brochures neatly arranged on the small desk next to the dresser. He scoots the chair back enough from it so he can open the middle drawer. Sure enough, there's a piece of stationary, an envelope, two postcards, and a pen in it. He sits down in the burgundy leather chair next to the desk and pages through the brochures.

The chair blends well with the beige textured-painted walls. The carpet, slightly worn but clean, matches the color of the walls. It has a variety of subtle burgundy and dark brown patterns. The comforter on the bed coordinates with the décor as do the wall decorations. "Looks like we'll have plenty to do for the next few days."

"For now, let's get in the pool." Stephanie trots out of the bathroom wearing her bikini and wiggles past Tony. She opens the door and races to the pool. Before Tony has barely made it out the doors and closed them, she flings her towel toward a chaise lounge and dives in swimming smoothly underwater to the other side.

Tony places his towel neatly next to hers and walks casually to the deep end where a spring board sits. He dives in and gently swims to Stephanie. They stay about mid pool against the wall enjoying the cool water and watching three kids splashing in the shallow end. "Those kids make me think of Rachel," Stephanie says. "I do hope she can have some of her own someday."

"With Jimmy that scumbag of a husband. He's nothing more than a dumbass kid himself."

"Maybe having kids will help him grow up." Stephanie splashes water in his face. "Besides, we'll be having our own, too, you know."

"Not until we get you out of debt, babe. Don't even think about it until then."

On that note, Stephanie backstrokes to the other edge, pulls herself out of the pool, quickly dries off, and stretches out on the chaise lounge for a bit of sunning. "After this week," she says to herself, "it may be sooner than you think."

Tony waits for about a minute before slowly making his way underwater back and forth for three laps side to side. Sensing enough time has passed, he pulls himself out of the pool to join Stephanie for some quiet relaxation. He knows Stephanie wants a baby as soon as possible, but he cannot fathom the prospect with all the money she owes.

A few minutes later, a large hairy tarantula creeps out of the grass and heads for Stephanie's chair. Tony notices and watches it intently. Stephanie lays on her back sunning. He gets up quietly and decides to carefully let it crawl onto his hand. He then places it next to her leg. He quietly sits back down and stretches out. Just before it decides to inch onto her leg, Tony whispers to Stephanie. "Don't move, Steph, there's a huge tarantula getting ready to crawl on your leg."

"Oh yeah, sure. Nice try, though."

"No, seriously. It's huge and hairy and fixing to get on your leg. You need to move slowly so I can knock it away."

Stephanie gives in and looks. Sure enough there sits a tarantula on the chair with her. She screams and jumps out of the chair. The kids in the pool turn to look at what's going on and see it, too. They scream, scurry out of the water, run to grab their towels, and huddle in the far corner.

Tony laughs and reaches over to let the tarantula crawl onto his hand. "It's OK everybody, it's harmless.

"Harmless, how do you know it's harmless?" Stephanie shrieks as she backs away taking tiny steps.

"From that stupid saucer men from Mars Indiana Jones movie. Don't you remember that scene when Mutt and Indiana went into the cave?"

"What scene? What are you talking about?"

"You know, the bigger the tarantula the better."

Stephanie doesn't get the reference and just wants Tony to get the tarantula the hell away from her. "You scared those kids, too, shame of you."

Tony sets the tarantula back into the shady grass from where it emerged, and assures the kids it's OK for them to get back in the water. He lays back down in his chair and gives Stephanie an apologetic look. She settles back into her chair. "I'll get you for this," she warns Tony playfully. "You just wait."

Twenty minutes pass before they decide they've had enough sun. They head back to their room. They take a quick shower together and enjoy putting on some of their new clothes. While Stephanie applies her makeup, Tony once again sits down in the leather chair and looks through the magazine describing all the shore excursions. “I see six possibilities for what we can do the next couple of days.”

Stephanie walks out of the bathroom applying blush to her cheeks. “I definitely want to go snorkeling, first thing.”

“There’s one in here.”

“Read it to me.”

“Convenient meeting location close to your Costa Maya cruise ship terminal. English speaking certified shore excursion guides and staff. Snorkeling at two of Costa Maya's best reefs. Best Price Guarantee.”

“How much is it.”

“Uh, only $49.99 per person.”

“Wow. Is that all. What else does it say?”

“All gear is included. Your snorkel guide will get you fitted and show you how it all works before escorting you into the water. During your trip, you will visit two beautiful areas of our reef. The average depth is six to 12 feet and you will be under the watchful eye of one of our guides. You will spend about 30 minutes at each stop before heading back to the beach. Water and soft drinks are provided during the excursion."

"Make it so."

"What time do you want to book; 8:30, 10:30, or 12:30?"

"10:30, that way we have a chance to eat some breakfast."

"Aye, Captain."

What else is there?"

"A paddleboat excursion, SCUBA diving, or a private beach club."

"Nothing about zip lining?"

"Not that I have seen so far."

"A couple of those things sound like fun. I bet there's probably more stuff to do, too."

"We'll ask Evelin when we go down for dinner."

I'm almost ready. Give me about five more minutes."

As soon as they open their door, they can smell the aromas coming from the restaurant just down the hall and across from the lobby. The inn offers two eating choices; an informal Senor Frog's outside by the garden, or a more formal Bone Fish Restaurant inside. Stephanie and Tony decide to check out the inside dining room. The restaurant contains beautifully set tables covered with blue overlay cloths over a white table cloth. Centerpieces of tall tropical flowers in glass vases anchor each table. On top of every plate perches a meticulously folded napkin.

Not too hungry because of their lunch, they munch on a generous appetizer portion of flour tortillas which they dip in a mole (mo-lay) sauce. Accompanied by fresh coconut juice, the sauce contains rich chocolate blended with a variety of medium to hot peppers and spices. It fills them rather quickly.

After dinner they take a relaxing walk then settle in their room for a quiet evening of TV viewing. They watch the *Star Trek: Into Darkness* movie and fall asleep during *Frozen*.

10

The bright morning begins with a pot of hot coffee and a heaping plate full of chilaquiles, fried tortilla pieces simmered in a spicy salsa and served with scrambled eggs. Stephanie and Tony stuff themselves more than usual and decide the 10-minute walk to the tourist area might be a good idea.

As they approach they see the familiar tourist village sight of shops with all their festive colors and hear the familiar beat of native music. The Dolphin Discovery quickly catches Tony's eyes and ears. The splashing of water, the singing of dolphins, and the applauding of people lead him toward the exhibit. "I wanna go. I wanna see. I wanna do." Tony eggs on Stephanie with his begging little boy voice.

A crowd of nearly 30 people gather around the ocean water exhibit to gleefully watch the paying customers interact with the dolphins. Called a dolphinarium the pool complete with a sandy-coated bottom serves as a habitat for bottle-nosed dolphins. After a 30-minute wait in line and the customary orientation session with trainers, Stephanie and Tony get their chance to play with the dolphins. Stephanie gets a kiss and a hug from Picabo, the larger of two featured dolphins on display for this morning session. Tony gets a handshake from Picabo's son Squirt. The two dolphins perform a couple of jumps and swimming acts before settling in for a game of catch. The game quickly turns into keep away much to the delight of the spectators with Squirt gently pushing away Stephanie whenever Picabo tosses the ball her way.

The encounter lasts about 15 minutes with the last five minutes saved for free time with the dolphins in the adjacent pool area. As Stephanie and Tony exit the pool the dolphins on cue beg for food. The session ends with them gladly gulping down the fish of their labors. They thank Stephanie and Tony by splashing them with their fins and singing for joy.

With no thoughts of Cooter and Hayes, Snake, Rachel, her parents, or even her school kids, Stephanie heads for the shopping area to kill some time before departure for their scheduled excursion of the day, a coral reef snorkeling experience followed by a visit to a private beach. Tony follows her about two steps behind reminding her that they have only about 30 minutes before the excursion leaves.

As calm and relaxing as the catamaran ride out to the coral reef is, the snorkeling turns into a harrowing adventure that nearly ends in disaster. The boat with 28 anxious tourists slowly maneuvers into position and stops after the 45-minute ride. A ride highlighted by watching a pair of dolphins that swim the last few minutes along the port bow. Two crewmates who sit on the bow for the ride inform everyone that in addition to watching the dolphins, they should also watch for stingrays loitering around the boat once it stops.

Three crew members already in the water who arrived minutes earlier to scope out the sight signal to the boat captain that several snapping sea turtles have congregated near the reef. Ordinarily no problem if one or two stray into the area during a snorkeling excursion, but a large group of snorkelers can easily agitate a group of sea turtles. It happens infrequently, but snorkelers have suffered injuries from foolishly approaching sea turtles during mating season or as they feed.

Since the excursion policies clearly indicate that swimmers snorkel at their own risk, the crew members take extra caution to monitor the site and warn participants to not approach the sea turtles. This works when everybody listens, but sometimes not everybody does.

Everybody on board who plans on snorkeling puts on their fins, blows up their personal flotation devices, and familiarizes themselves with their masks. A few, however, change their minds at the last minute and elect to stay onboard.

The first group off the boat, two snorkelers who meet the criteria of having snorkeled at least three times, follow their leader and easily head farther out to sea. The second group, experienced swimmers who have snorkeled at least twice, follow their leader and explore at a bit slower pace and not as far out. The third group, first- and second-time snorkelers and even a few non swimmers, ease into the water last. They stay close to the boat with their leader until all feel comfortable maneuvering in their fins and masks with their personal flotation devices tugging softly at their necks. Once the leader feels assured all have acclimated, he leads them slowly away from the boats stern.

One gentleman panics a bit and needs immediate help getting back on the boat. Two ladies flail about for a few seconds and then finally get their bearings. Everybody else easily gets into a rhythm satisfying the leader that the snorkeling may now begin. Stephanie and Tony start out in the middle of the pack of this group but quickly advance to the front.

A school of foot-long white fish swim just in front of Stephanie and Tony as they work their way with the group along the port side of the boat and out to sea. They explore the red formation of the coral reef less than 12 feet below them. The shapes and sizes amaze them as do the variety of fish; some black, some yellow, and some transparent. Even the fauna has an alien-world quality to it that impresses the eye. Less than five minutes into the exploring, group three leader signals suddenly for everybody to turn around and head back to the boat. A couple of snapping sea turtles have approached the group a little too close for comfort.

The two ladies who had trouble as they got into the water, who apparently hadn't listened well during the orientation, and who didn't catch the leaders signal to turn around, keep swimming toward the turtles. Group three leader stays with his swimmers and knows he doesn't need to signal to one of the earlier arriving crew members who guards the perimeter on the port side to come help the two ladies.

He gets between the ladies and the sea turtles trying to protect them from an improbable but possible attack. If the sea turtles attack and start snapping, not only the two ladies but the crewmember risk serious injury. Instead of remaining calm, as everybody had been told several times during orientation, the two ladies begin flailing again and quickly use up all their strength. Upon seeing this group three leader takes off his mask and implores everybody to calmly swim back to the boat. He quickly heads out to help the other crewmember with the two ladies.

Two other crewmembers, who stay on the boat with the guests that decide not to snorkel jump in to help with keeping group three together and on track back to the boat. Group two, about 50 yards farther out, heads back to the boat circling around to starboard as does group one who have managed to explore nearly 100 yards from the boat.

Suddenly the awe of seeing stingrays and dolphins loitering around the boat turns into dread for the few people who stay onboard. They fear that the two ladies may drown or could still get attacked. Both ladies lose their masks and gulp mouthfuls of water as they scream. With their eyes closed and in panic mode they think the crewmembers trying to save them are the snapping sea turtles.

Stephanie and Tony, both excellent swimmers, resist the urge to stay in the water to offer to help. They get back on the boat with the rest of the group at the urging of the boat captain. He has come down from the bridge to the stern to help everybody climb safely back on the boat, not an easy task for many of the swimmers who aren't used to wearing fins.

Finally, group three leader and the other crew members get the ladies under control. Even though they have on personal floatation devices, the captain throws life preservers toward them so they can be pulled more quickly back to the boat.

Once onboard the two ladies receive basic first aid and soon cough up the water in their lungs. Moments later they sit up and group three leader drapes dry towels around them. He talks to them until he's assured they are calm and uninjured. He then motions the thumbs up to the captain who turns the boat around and speeds back to shore zipping past the stop at the private island. The usual leisurely 45-minute ride takes only a speedy 30 minutes, half an hour that goes by with the deafening silence of 28 tourists, two of which sit exhausted realizing they are lucky to be alive.

The experience jolts Stephanie back to reality. Thoughts of all the money she owes Snake flood her mind. Rachel's miscarriages and questionable marriage distract her. Even concerns about her aging parents and the prospect that they will be gone someday haunt her. She realizes that once spring break ends and Tony and she return to the states, unpleasant realities await.

The boat docks. Two of the four first aid personnel standing by quickly board to aid the two ladies. Still looking pale and confused, each has her blood pressure, pulse, and heart rate checked. By the time the other two first aid personnel carry stretchers on board, the ladies have also had their ears, eyes, noses, and mouths checked. In a few minutes they are carried off the boat and taken to the first aid station for further evaluation. The rest of the tourists then disembark, still maintaining a somber silence.

Stephanie and Tony slowly walk back to the hotel in the heat of the day. Tony, sensing Stephanie's obvious worried deportment, tries to engage her in conversation. He points to a row of shrubs off to the right, "I wonder what kind of flowers those are?"

"Don't know, don't care," Stephanie mumbles without looking up.

"They look like lantana to me, the orange ones over there, especially."

Stephanie again doesn't look. Instead she stops and looks up at the sky. "What am I going to do about paying back Snake? What am I going to do about helping Rachel? What am I going to do about Mom and Dad?

"I don't know, Steph, I really don't. But at least we don't have to worry about Snake's two thugs."

"Oh really," Stephanie says. "How do you know that they might not be waiting for us right now at the hotel?"

"Because they are in jail up in Cozumel, you know, with Captain Gonzalez and all his glory."

"Maybe so, maybe not."

"Steph, honey, we're OK. Don't let what happened to those two ladies get to you too much."

"How can you say that? They could have drowned."

"Yes, I know, but they didn't. Let it go."

"Easy for you to say," Stephanie kicks a rock and then proceeds to lurch forward at a quickened pace leaving Tony two steps behind again.

When they arrive at the hotel, Evelin greets them with a big smile. She starts to say something, but Tony raises his hand toward her and shakes his head.

"Not now, Evelin," Tony says to her. "Two ladies almost drowned while snorkeling and Stephanie is still pretty shaken up about it."

"Oh my," Evelin says putting both hands over her mouth. "Are they alright?"

Tony assures her with a quick nod, "I'll tell you all about it later." He hustles down the hall to unlock the room for Stephanie.

She sits on the bed and starts to cry. "Tony, she says while wiping tears from her eyes with her hands, "what did that security guard from the Gem mean when he said he wasn't sure we could get back on the cruise ship here? What if he's right?"

"I don't know that either," he answers. "When we go back into town, I'll try to find out. I'm sure there are some authorities or officials here that I can talk to."

Stephanie stretches out on the bed for a nap. She's upset and needs some time to herself. Tony senses this and decides to use this time to fill in Evelin on the snorkeling calamity and ask who he can talk to about their predicament. Evelin semi-assures him that they should have no problem getting back on the Swedish Gem Friday, but suggests he walk back into port to talk to the personnel at the Ruby, another one of the SCA ships docked for the day.

"Good idea," he says to Evelin. I'll do that right now, thanks."

A few passengers drift on and off the Ruby, some finished with their morning excursions and some just heading out for their afternoon excursions. Ruby personnel have wet towels soaked in mango-laced water for the tourists ready to re board. Local personnel, in native garb, sing, dance, and offer photo opportunities for the tourists disembarking.

Tony explains the predicament to the guard manning the first scanner where passengers show their room keys to disembark and re board the ship. He shares only the relevant details about missing the Gem, not having passports, and hoping to re board here Friday. The guard listens patiently, nodding frequently maintaining a neutral expression on her face. With a distinct Australian accent and a slight smile, she tells him that they should not have a problem if they have their room key and a driver's license. "Let me double check, though," she says. "I'll call the Head Security Officer."

A few minutes later a large man in a meticulously pressed white uniform approaches. He shakes Tony's hand with a firm grip. Tony can feel the strength in his large fingers. In a thick, rugged French accent he introduces himself, "Bonjour monsieur, I am Chappelle, Head Security Officer, what can I do for you?"

Tony once again explains the necessary details. After a formal reply in which he cites a few policies and procedures, Chappelle pats Tony on the shoulder and assures him that the Gem will gladly welcome them back on board. "I hope you enjoy the rest of your time here and have a pleasant cruise back to New Orleans."

Chappelle acknowledges the guard with a tip of his hat and heads around the corner. Tony notices the guards name tag and gives her a pleasant, "Thank you, Chelsea."

She responds with "G'day."

When Tony arrives back at the hotel room he finds Stephanie still asleep on the bed. Tears have caused her eye makeup to run down her face. She stirs and Tony tells her to stay there. He goes into the bathroom and wets a wash cloth. He sits on the bed next to her and wipes her face. "We're good to go, Steph," he says. "I talked with the Head Security Officer of another Swedish cruise ship docked in port."

"Are you sure?" Stephanie whispers as she stretches and yawns.

"Absolutely," Tony answers in his best Rocky Balboa imitation.

Stephanie smiles and gives him a big hug. "Let's go for a swim."

At the pool they meet a couple from Canada. Not too eager to talk much and more interested in clinging to each other in the pool, they do manage to introduce themselves as Randy and Terri Burton from Winnipeg, Manitoba. "We're on our honeymoon, just got here about an hour ago."

"She looks about six months pregnant and both of them can't be a day over 17," Stephanie whispers to Tony."

Terri compliments Stephanie on the purple in her hair and how it matches her bikini. Stephanie thanks her and asks, "Is it a boy or a girl?"

"He's a boy, Roger Daniel," Terri answers.

"Uh, Phillip Dean," Randy quickly adds.

Terri curls her nose and gives him a quick slap on the arm. "No way, Jose," she chides him, "we agreed on Roger Daniel." As she dunks him he manages to just get out, "Phillip Dean."

Stephanie and Tony laugh then swim off to give the young couple space to splash about. "I hope we have the chance soon to argue about baby names," Stephanie says. "I hope Rachel does, too."

The rest of the late afternoon passes quietly and it's soon time for dinner. After showers and a change into fresh shorts and t-shirts, Stephanie and Tony head for the dining room. Over generous portions of shrimp steamed in white wine and garlic, they engage in a lively discussion about the upcoming release of the previously unknown first novel of Harper Lee, *Go Set a Watchman.*

"I can't wait to read more about Scout, Jem, Dill, and all the rest of them," Tony says. "It should be a hoot."

"I don't know," Stephanie replies. "I've read that it gets pretty intense about the civil rights uprisings of the 1950s."

"Yes, but to know what's in this book that prompted Harper Lee's editor to encourage her to put this version aside and write about their childhood in the 1930s," Tony explains." That's what intrigues me."

"I must admit I am curious about what Atticus is like as an old man," Stephanie wonders. "I hope Calpurnia is still alive."

With that discussion topic ended over an after-dinner cup of coffee, Stephanie and Tony settle into their room and spend the rest of the evening uneventfully reading in bed until they fall asleep.

Their final day in Costa Maya flies by with a morning excursion of stand up paddle boating, an afternoon excursion of SCUBA diving, and an evening of dining and dancing. Feeling exhausted and anxious to get on with their cruise in the morning, they have no trouble getting to sleep. Tomorrow will be a big day for them, but not the way they expect.

11

Sounds outside the patio door of their hotel room awakens Tony. He looks first at Stephanie who isn't stirring and then stares at the red digital display of the bedside clock until his eyes focus. It reads 5:17 a.m.

He stumbles out of bed and opens the drapes. Two chaise lounges whisk by on their sides and bash into two others that have pushed against a cabana. He opens the door and gets slammed by a gust of wind that nearly knocks him over. Stephanie wakes up and hollers, "What's going on?"

"A bit of a windy morning, that's all," Tony assures her. "Let's go back to sleep."

***

The Swedish Gem approaches Costa Maya from the south. It has been to Belize City, Belize, and Roatan Island, Honduras, all without Stephanie and Tony or Cooter and Hayes. It's scheduled to dock at 8 a.m., but concerns raise on the bridge.

Rough seas cause the ship to rock a bit more than usual and passengers stirring early notice it. At 6:45 a.m., a familiar voice makes her first announcement of the day. "Good morning this is Caroline your Cruise Director." But instead of her usual fanfare about the latest port, she offers another message.

"The Captain has been in discussion with the Costa Maya Port Authority for the past hour about their concerns that high winds and waves may prevent us from docking on time. We have been asked to maintain our position and await further word."

After a brief pause, Caroline continues. "The Captain assures me that he is doing everything he can to convince the Port Authority officials that we can dock safely even if we have to wait until the winds and waves reduce to below minimum safety standards."

The announcement wakes up Clark and Margie, one of the couples Stephanie and Tony played table games with in the ships casino on the first days of the cruise to Cozumel. Margie nudges Clark, "Did you hear that?"

"Yes, dear, I did."

Margie scolds him, "I told you we should have scheduled a Mayan ruins tour earlier in the cruise. The one thing I really wanted to do."

"You don't know that we won't get to dock."

Margie keeps at him, "We should have gone to Tulum."

"Let's wait and see," Clark heads to the bathroom.

"If we don't dock, we don't get to go to the Mayan ruins at Chacchoben."

"Yes, dear, I know."

"The one thing I really wanted to do."

By 7:15 a.m. they make their way up the elevator from their deck five cabin to the buffet on deck 12 for breakfast. They "Happy, happy, washy, washy" on the way in. Margie finds a table next to the window. She opens two napkins and spreads out the silverware to mark the table as taken. She heads for the beverage kiosk to pour a cup of coffee and a glass of orange juice for each of them. She returns them to the table and joins Clark in the buffet line.

He's nearly through the line stuffing his plate with his usual morning fare; two scoops of scrambled eggs, two scoops of hash browns, four strips of bacon and two biscuits all smothered with white gravy.

Margie stands at the omelet station ordering her usual custom-made choice filled with onions, cheese, and tomatoes. She adds two strips of bacon, a small spoonful of hash browns, and a single biscuit. She carefully tears open the biscuit and ladles on some gravy. She places a small cherry pastry on an open spot she leaves on her plate.

Both walk carefully to their table, as does everybody else, as the ship continues to rock noticeably. "Look at those waves," Margie says. "We're not going to dock."

The Costa Maya coastline can be seen in the distance off the port bow, but mostly all the eye can see are miles and miles of choppy waves rhythmically yet annoyingly rocking north to south.

Clark and Margie add milk and sweetener to their coffee and take their first sips of the morning just as "Good morning this is Caroline your Cruise Director," blares once again over the speakers.

"Due to continuing weather conditions the Costa Maya Port Authority has closed the port and disallowed all cruise ships to dock today. The Captain offers his deepest apologies."

Again a pause followed by, "I'll be back in a few minutes with a schedule of fun and exciting shipboard activities for you to enjoy as we head back to New Orleans at half speed with an extra day at sea."

Disappointed, Clark and Margie eat their breakfast and chat idly until she has a sudden thought. "I wonder whatever happened to that nice couple from Arkansas that didn't get back on the ship in Cozumel."

***

Stephanie and Tony finally get up at 7:30 a.m. and can't wait to get going. They shower quickly, fill their backpacks, check out, say "adios" to Evelin, and walk out the hotel door. They instantly get sand blown in their eyes before they can get on their sunglasses. "At least we'll be walking downwind," Tony says as they turn right.

After a walk with the gusty wind blowing sand on their backs, and knocking Stephanie's hat off twice, they approach the tourist village. It sits strangely quiet. They walk a little bit further and notice no ships docked. Tony looks at his watch. "That's strange, it's nearly 8:00 a.m. You'd think the place would be bustling by now."

"I'm getting a bad feeling about this," Stephanie says. "It's almost like we're in *The Langoliers*."

They walk into the first bar they see and spot the bartender covering tables and chairs. "What's going on?" Tony asks.

"No ships today, too windy, amigos," he says.

"What do you mean exactly?" Stephanie asks.

"Waves too high, port closed, no ships today."

"But we're supposed to board the Swedish Gem here today," Stephanie pleads. "We've been waiting all week."

"Sorry, not my circus, not my monkeys, adios."

The bartender, in a hurry to leave his establishment now that it's safe and secure from the weather, leads them outside. "Go find help that way," he says. "Look for green and yellow uniforms."

With that he jumps on his bicycle and pedals against the wind. He struggles to make headway and decides quickly to get off the bike and walk it. Stephanie and Tony walk onward hoping to find some Swedish Cruise Adventures personnel. About 50 yards downwind they see a green and yellow banner flapping on the front of a makeshift pavilion.

A man in a green and yellow uniform stands just inside. He holds a walkie-talkie to his right ear and has his hand over his left ear to help block out the noise of the wind and waves. Next to him standing behind a table a similarly dressed lady tries to keep a pile of papers and files organized. "Excuse me ma'am, Tony says to her. "We need some information about the Swedish Gem."

"Sorry, she not dock today, port authority close port, too windy, waves too choppy."

"Yes, we realize that, but we are in a bit of a jam."

Tony gives her a brief rundown of their dilemma. She listens attentively, but offers nothing more than, "maybe Torres here can help you."

"I heard your story," Torres says. "May I see your room keys and passports, please?

"We don't have our passports. We left them in our cabin on the ship back in Cozumel," Tony offers.

"Oh my, that's going to be a problem," Torres replies. "Do you have any other identification besides your room keys?"

"Just our drivers' licenses," Stephanie says.

They give them to Torres. "Well, Stephanie and Tony Shafer from Arkansas USA, you need to talk to a port agent. I'll walk you to the Port Authority office. It's not far."

"Thank you," offers Stephanie. "Does this happen very often that the port gets closed because of high seas?"

"This is the first time here as far as I know," answers Torres. "I'm just as surprised as you are."

Lopez the lady adds, "I heard it happened in Costa Rica a couple of years ago. Ship stranded all day."

"Let's go, folks," Torres says as he walks out with them. "I hope they can help you. Sorry we can't do anything for you."

Led by Torres, Stephanie and Tony tackle the wind once more. In a couple of minutes they walk into a sweltering office bustling with activity, so much so that they sit and wait for 20 minutes before a robust woman with sweat beads on her forehead approaches them. She plops down in the seat next to Tony.

"Good morning, we are Stephanie and Tony Shafer."

"Hello, my name is Anna-Maria Martinez. How may I help you?"

Tony once again tells the tale emphasizing that they need to get to New Orleans by Sunday so they can drive back to Arkansas. Stephanie has to turn back into Ms. Shafer the teacher for Monday morning and Tony must go back on restaurant manager duty by the lunch shift.

"Si, I understand," Martinez says taking a deep breath. "Let me make a phone call to the American Consulate in

Quintana Roo. I know someone there who can probably help you."

In a few minutes she returns with a frazzled, but positive expression on her face. She explains that they can get a temporary passport from the American Consulate office and make arrangements there for a flight back to the U.S.

"That's great," Tony says almost jumping out of his chair to shake her hand.

"Not so fast, amigos," Martinez warns. "It's not so easy."

"Uh, oh," Stephanie grunts. "Here we go again."

"You have a rental car?" Martinez asks.

"We did," answers Tony, "that's how we got here from Cozumel, but we turned it in a couple of days ago."

Martinez tells them that they must rent a car again and drive two hours to the American Consulate in Quintana Roo, the state capital. "There you find the Consular

Section and ask for Senor Diaz. Since its Friday," she adds, "you must get there before three o'clock. They often close early for the weekend. Bus will take too long and make many stops."

Having no other real choice, they follow Martinez's directions to the car rental and pile into another little yellow Chevy Spark for a drive back inland toward Chacchoben and beyond.

Stephanie spends the first 30 minutes of the bumpy ride on Hwy 293 to the state capital with pen and paper adding up all the incidental costs they have incurred during this free cruise week. "Maybe we should have gone to Vegas like we originally talked about," she says after adding up all the meals, hotel stays, car rentals, clothes purchases, and police payola. "Now we have to pay for temporary passports and plane tickets."

Tony pats her on the leg. "Yeah, but think of all the stories you can tell the kids when you get back to school."

They stop only once on the way to Quintana Roo. Stephanie spots an old man sitting in the shade near the intersection of Hwy 307 and 293 selling wild mangos, oranges, papayas, and tomatoes out of the back of his pickup truck. A panting dog that looks about as old as the man lies sleeping next to him. The old man fans himself to not only try to stay cool, but to fend off the flies and gnats hovering over the dog.

Tony agrees to stop but tells Stephanie she must hurry. She does coming back to the car in less than five minutes with a shoe box full of mangos and oranges.

By 2:15 p.m. they pull into Quintana Roo and easily find the Consulate following Martinez's directions. Once inside they look for the Consular Section sign and ask to speak with Senor Diaz.

"Si, I am Diaz. You are Americanos from Costa Maya?"

"Si, I mean yes, yes we are," Tony says. "Anna-Maria Martinez from the Port Authority office there sent us."

"Ah, sweet Anna-Maria," Diaz sighs, "we have been good friends for many years."

Once again Tony tells the story of the past week.

Diaz responds with "quite an adventure."

"Yes, quite an adventure," Stephanie says smiling. "Now, how much is it going to cost to get temporary passports and how long will it take?"

"If you have $500, then I can have them ready in about an hour."

"We don't have enough cash for that."

"You may put it on a charge card," Diaz answers quickly. "Same as for making your flight reservation."

"Do we catch a flight here to get back to the states?" Tony wants to know.

"Oh no, senor, you must drive to Cancun. There you take non-stop flight to New Orleans."

"Cancun," Stephanie bellows, "Are you kidding me? That's north of Cozumel."

"Si, Senora, a five-hour drive from here."

Stephanie is not amused. "Oh for Pete's sake, this is turning into a nightmare."

Sensing the right time to keep his mouth shut, Diaz takes his time to get the paperwork started for the temporary passports. He notices out of the corner of his eye that Stephanie heads for the restroom and Tony for the water fountain. Given this short reprieve, he decides to make this rush job an even 'rusher' job. In fact, by the time Stephanie returns from powdering her nose he has already made their flight reservations.

"Please fill out these forms, then I take pictures of you. Your flight itinerary prints even as we speak."

Wait," says Tony. "We haven't decided on which flight to take."

"Senor, there is only one flight from Cancun to New Orleans tomorrow. You take that one or you no go at all."

Diaz hands Tony the printouts. They're booked on an 11:31 a.m.–1:37 p.m. flight tomorrow morning. It costs $183 per person, less than the cost of their temporary passports. "A two-hour flight over the Gulf is better than a 38-hour drive around it," he says. "Still you have long drive ahead of you, I make your passports now."

While Stephanie and Tony wait they discuss whether to drive straight through to Cancun late this afternoon and evening or to stop in Playa del Carmen for the night and go into Cancun in the morning.

"I just want to get this over with," Stephanie says. "No more stopovers, please. Let's just get there."

"I agree," says Tony once again patting her on the leg.

In less than an hour, as promised, Diaz hands them a pocket folder containing their temporary passports and flight itinerary. He asks them if the SCA personnel in Costa Maya told them how to get their belongings back after the Gem docks in New Orleans.

"No sir, no they didn't," Tony says. "As a matter of fact, I hadn't even thought about that."

"Me, neither," adds Stephanie giving Diaz a look of bewilderment. "Oh, geez."

"Let me make phone call for you. I will get details of what you need to do."

Stephanie and Tony realize that the three of them are the only ones left in the building. Well past 3 p.m., everyone else has left for the weekend. "We really appreciate you staying late to help us," Tony says to Diaz. "It looks pretty empty in here now."

"No problem," says Diaz. "But you are right. Except for security, everybody has vamoosed."

In a few minutes Diaz returns with more information for them. "Here is phone number for you to call when you get back to U.S.A. You talk to Amelia at SCA headquarters in Miami. Your belongings will be sent from New Orleans to Lost and Found there."

"Why can't we just get our stuff in New Orleans Sunday morning when the ship docks?" Stephanie asks.

"Rules, regulations, protocols, and procedures," Diaz answers. "You talk to Amelia about all that."

"How can we thank you," Tony says as he shakes Diaz hand."

"I know," says Stephanie. "I'll be right back."

She goes to the car and grabs the shoebox full of fruit. When she comes back in she offers Diaz a mango, a papaya, an orange, and a tomato. "I just bought them at a fruit stand back at the intersection 293 and 307."

"Oh, that must have been from Rojo," Diaz says happily. "Muchas gracias, many thanks. Did he still have that old dog with him?"

"Yes, fleas and all," Stephanie laughs.

"Adios, amigos. Thanks again for the fruit."

"Thank <u>you</u> very much, Senor Diaz," Stephanie says as she gives him a gentle hug.

"Oh senora, you have made my weekend."

By 4 p.m. Stephanie and Tony head once again for Hwy 307 for their hopefully uneventful and tolerable drive to

Cancun International Airport over five hours north by northeast.

12

While Stephanie and Tony's week in Costa Maya ends with them not being able to re board the Gem for a pleasant cruise back to New Orleans, and all the frustrations of trying to find a way out of Mexico, Cooter and Hayes's bleak week in the 'municipal facilities' in Cozumel ends with an eagerly accepted offer from Captain Gonzalez to get out in the sun and perform a few days' worth of community service. "You hombres may stay where you are for three more days, or you may spend them on the mainland outdoors in the glorious sun performing some light labor."

"What glorious light labor will we be doing exactly?" asks Cooter.

"Hush," Hayes implores him. "We don't care what it is, just let us out of this hell hole."

Gonzalez wryly smiles knowing that after four days in his jail cell, known as the Infierno Verde, that prisoners seldom turn down any opportunity to get out in the fresh air and sunlight, no matter how hot it is , what the labor involves, and where it is.

"Excellent, hombres, you must leave now to catch the boat. Come on out and after Monday you will be free of this jail."

"Catch the boat," Cooter says. "What do you mean? Where are we going?"

"To Playa del Carmen, on the mainland," Gonzalez replies.

"Wait a minute," adds Cooter.

Hayes once again tells him to hush. "We're good to go, Captain. We're definitely good to go."

Not only have Cooter and Hayes endured the misery of the jail itself, they have also been schooled all week long by the many embellished and long-winded stories from Captain Gonzalez about the history of Infierno Verde, which translates into English as 'Green Hell,' a name given to the original jail by political dissidents shipped to the remote, lush island in the early 1900s by then Mexican President Diaz.

The history lesson begins the same for all those unfortunates who take up temporary residence in the jail. During the 1860s reign of Maximillian, according to Gonzalez, Cozumel Island served as sort of a "Devil's Island" because of its isolated location and small population of about 400 people. Gonzalez even claims that in 1938 six prisoners escaped from the real Devil's Island and made their way to Cozumel as stowaways on a freighter.

"They lived out their lives here, and some of them still have family on the island."

Accompanied by two of Gonzalez's deputies, Cooter and Hayes survive the bumpy boat ride to the mainland and spend four hours picking up trash along the shoreline. After a 30-minute break at noon, they spend four more hours sweeping the adjacent sidewalks. "Oh, well," Hayes realizes at the end of the day, "better than rotting in that jail listening to Gonzalez going on and on."

Cooter agrees. "I wish we could get word to Snake, though. He'd give Gonzalez a run for his money."

"I'd like to see that," Hayes laughs as sweat drips from his forehead. "King Kong vs. Godzilla."

"Man, I'm so damn thirsty. I wish we got something better to drink than just water."

"I know. I have a hankering for a snow cone."

"A what?"

"You heard me, a snow cone."

"I think being cooped up in the jail and having to listen to Gonzalez's stories whenever he's in the office has gotten to you, my friend. An iced cold beer, yes; a snow cone, that's just plain weird."

"I'm telling you right now, I'd give five dollars for a grape snow ice."

"Well, it's not going to happen here, so forget it."

With another wave of cruise ships due to port next week, Cooter and Hayes join a dozen other local workers sprucing up the area for the thousands of tourists who will disembark for their shore excursions starting again Monday morning. The economy depends on this peak time of the season. Nothing else comes close to attracting tourists to the area like the cruise ship season, not even the PGA Tour golf tournament held at nearby El Cameleon Golf Club at Mayakoba in November.

While they work all day and will all weekend in the exhausting heat, Cooter and Hayes prefer it to remaining in the jail during the long, hot days. In fact, the time they spend talking with the local workers intrigues Cooter to the point of considering staying permanently in Cozumel, particularly since Hayes and he failed in their "enforcer" efforts toward Stephanie and Tony. Cooter and Hayes have not contacted Snake since their arrest, and they have no intention of doing so. Any update would not bode well for them.

In fact, having talked throughout the morning and afternoon with other members on work detail about their jobs and living on the island or in Playa del Carmen, Cooter sprouts a crazy idea. "Hayes, let's open a snow cone stand."

"Seriously?!"

"You heard me, let's stay down here and open our own business."

"Are you out of your mind, Cooter? You've been in the sun too long."

"Why not. Tell me one reason why we shouldn't do this."

"I don't know, it just sounds stupid."

"Just wait until Tuesday, then. I'll show you what I mean."

Cooter adds one last thought for Hayes. "Besides, do you want to face Snake after we have botched this job?"

"Good point," Hayes admits. "Maybe a snow cone stand isn't a bad idea."

Guards Alonzo and Alvarez lead Cooter and Hayes along with the rest of the work detail to a shady area where they have a meal of fresh fruit and vegetables. Afterward, the local workers disperse while Cooter and Hayes led by the guards head for the boat to ride back to the island and jail.

13

Making only a pit stop at a travel plaza in Playa del Carmen for gas and a restroom break, Stephanie and Tony plan to zip through town as quickly as they can. "Reckon Cooter and Hayes are still out on the island in jail?" Tony asks as he gets out of the car and stretches.

"I suppose so, don't you?" Stephanie replies. "Not interested in finding out, though."

"That's for sure."

As Tony fills the gas tank his curiosity gets an unexpected answer. He spots two uniformed guards and two what he assumes are prisoners wearing orange work duty vests walking toward him from across the road about 50 feet away. Something about the two prisoners in the vests catches his eye.

By the time Stephanie returns to the car, the foursome has made it directly across the street from them. "Stephanie," Tony says just above a whisper, "look at those guys across the street. Do you see what I see?"

"I see two guys in orange vests and two guys in police uniforms, so what?"

"Look more closely at the two guys in front. Recognize them?"

"Why would I recog …" Stephanie stops mid word. "Oh shit."

"Oh shit, for sure." They both duck behind the car. "It's Snake's two thugs."

"What the hell are they doing here on the mainland?"

"I don't know, Steph, but there they are."

"Must be some sort of work detail," she infers. "And in this heat."

"Stay down, we'll wait until they walk well past us."

"Hey officers," Hayes announces. "I need to take a piss."

"I could, too" says Cooter.

"Too bad, keep moving," growls Alvarez. "No time for that now."

"I don't care," Hayes growls back. "I need to go."

"Me, too," Cooter repeats.

The two guards look at each other and decide to let them. "All right," Alvarez says. "Head over to that travel plaza across the street, and make it snappy."

Stephanie and Tony both ease up to sneak a peek expecting to see them walking away. But instead, here they come. Cooter spots Stephanie and Tony first. He cannot believe it. "Well, what have we here?"

Hayes see them now, too. "What do you know about that? Fancy running into you two."

The guards grab Cooter and Hayes pushing them away. "Don't get any stupid ideas," Alonzo warns.

"Officers," Tony says, "we are ..."

"We know who you are," Alonzo interrupts. "Get in your car and get out of here, now. We have these two well in hand."

"We're not done with you," Cooter threatens Stephanie. "You owe a lot of money to Snake, and you owe it real soon."

"Wouldn't want anything really bad to happen to your pretty little wife," Hayes adds.

"That's enough," Alonzo barks. Alvarez and he both tighten their grip.

Alonzo repeats his order to Stephanie and Tony. "Go, you two, now. Get out of here."

This time Stephanie and Tony do not hesitate. Cooter and Hayes do not resist.

Once calmed down and well out of town, during the last hour of their drive up to Cancun, Stephanie and Tony finish the rest of the oranges and mangos, share a package of cheese crackers, and a drink a bottle of Coke Light. By the time they arrive at a Comfort Inn just past the Cancun International Airport and near the car rental drop off, they feel like they have been "rode hard and put up wet."

"As my Grammy used to say, that drive was too fer and snaky." Stephanie pulls herself out of the car.

"Yeah, my grandmother used to say clear out to Gobbler's Nob and back." Tony again stretches his back. "Oh, well, we're finally here."

"No more drama, please," Stephanie says. "I've had enough for one week."

The next morning finds Stephanie and Tony dropping off the Chevy at the airport car rental and shuttling to the terminal by 8:30 a.m. No way do they want to risk having to rush or being late anticipating that having their temporary passports and only backpacks as their luggage will cause suspicion and delay. Diaz had suggested to them that they arrive no later than 8:30 a.m., and for them to be ready for anything and anybody that may seem uncomfortable at both check in and security.

Surprisingly, things go rather quickly and pleasantly for them. Their temporary passports create only a second and third glance from both airline and security personnel. Them not having luggage to check prompts a bit of concern, but only to the point of both of them being asked to step aside for an extra pat down at security as well as having their back packs opened and inspected.

By 9:45 a.m. they finish the post 9/11 ordeal all air passengers have gotten so used to over the past 14 years that memories of not having the procedures don't even exist for many. They walk leisurely through the terminal toward their gate keeping an eye out for a good place to have breakfast. Stephanie spots a familiar sign. "Bingo," she says, "There's a TGI Fridays."

"Let's have some normal eggs, bacon, toast, and coffee," she says.

"You go right ahead. I'm in the mood for pancakes with hot maple syrup and sausage."

Enjoying their last meal in Mexico, they finish with a toast clinking their coffee cups, "Next spring break, Vegas," Tony says.

"I don't know," Stephanie adds. "I really would like to see Belize and Honduras."

They finish their walk to the gate and find two empty seats among the growing crowd of passengers with their various carry-on items. Its 10:40 a.m. and anxious passengers start to line up by the gate in anticipation of the boarding announcements beginning soon. Stephanie and Tony relax in their seats. They like to board last so they can avoid the usual crowding, cramping, and complaining that always occurs as passengers jockey for overhead bins and struggle to both find and get in their seats.

A lady sitting in the row behind Stephanie taps her on the shoulder. "Did I hear you say in the restaurant that you'd like to go to Belize and Honduras?"

Stephanie turns around to find an attractive middle-aged woman smiling at her. "I didn't mean to eavesdrop, but my husband and I have been to Roatan Island and Belize City several times on a cruise."

"Oh, really, Stephanie acknowledges, "on Swedish?"

"Yes, we've gone three years in a row. We love it."
Her husband puts down his newspaper and joins in the conversation. "Next year, we're going on an Alaskan cruise."

"Well," Stephanie sys, "we were supposed to visit both Belize and Honduras this week on our cruise, but we got a bit sidetracked."

"To say the least." Tony now joins in. "It's a long, complicated story."

The boarding begins and as they finish introducing themselves, the line starts to move evenly. The husband

and wife hail from Overland Park, a suburb of southwest Kansas City, on the Kansas side. Cassie and Max Burnett, they're retired college professors enjoying their pensions.

They get in line and Cassie says she hopes they can continue their talk on the plane. As the line dwindles to the last couple of passengers, Stephanie and Tony finally get up. They show their boarding passes and walk slowly through the jet bridge hoping the congestion eases by the time they get to door of the plane. It hasn't.

They worm their way to row 23, seats A and B. Cassie and Max wave at them from four rows back and across the aisle. Stephanie and Tony settle into their seats. Once everybody else does as well, Cassie asks one of the flight attendants to see if the two passengers in row 23, seats C and D would mind switching seats with them. Much to Stephanie and Tony's dismay, they're really not in the mood to chat all the way to New Orleans with strangers on a plane, the passengers across the aisle agree. Quickly four people and their stuff switch rows.

After the plane takes off, Cassie tells Stephanie and Tony about everything they missed seeing and doing in Belize

City. By the time the snack and beverage cart gets to their row about 30 minutes into the flight, Cassie moves on to her tales of Roatan Island.

"There's this park," she starts. It's called Gumbalimba. It is just a wonderful place to hike through."

She tells of exploring a manmade cave where pirates once stashed their booty. "There's an insectarium inside that's really fascinating."

"In fact," Max adds, "there's a framed case hanging on one of the walls with 26 butterflies mounted in it."

"Oh, really," nods Tony.

"How 'bout that," politely adds Stephanie.

"Yes, and what's amazing about it, a man spent 33 years finding a butterfly with each letter of the alphabet on its pattern. A to Z, each butterfly has a letter on it, clear as a bell."

"Imagine that," Tony says.

"Wow, 33 years, that's really something," Stephanie again adds politely.

"But that's not the best part," Cassie says leaning even further out into the aisle. "Wait until I tell you about the capuchin monkeys and the parrots."

Stephanie sighs and feigns a smile. Tony rolls his eyes.

"The monkeys jump right up on your shoulders and snuggle. What's really something, though, is how soft their fur feels and how good they smell."

"Really," says Stephanie. "They aren't nasty dirty?"

"Not at all, they're as sweet as any animal can be."

"But you better hold onto your hat, sunglasses, and bottles," Max adds. "Their quick little thieves, too."

Cassie shows them all the photos stored on her phone. "See this parrot," she says when she gets past all her monkey pictures. That prompts her to tell the tale of Bernie, the love struck parrot.

"He's 19 years old and sits on your shoulder, too. He loves to pose for pictures, see."

"How cute is that," says Stephanie.

"Pretty cool," Tony adds.

"But what's funny about him, he gets a day off once a week and you won't believe what he does."

"What? What?" Stephanie asks with feigned curiosity.

"Tell us. Tell us." Tony echoes. Stephanie punches him with her elbow.

"Every Monday, that's his day off, he flies straight to the Roatan airport eight miles away to visit his girlfriend."

"Seriously," Stephanie says.

"You're kidding, "Tony adds.

"He stays all day and his handler has to drive to pick him up. He won't fly back."

"That's quite story, indeed," Tony says as he looks at Stephanie and smiles. "It really is."

"For sure," she agrees.

"Well, thanks for telling us about what we missed in Belize and Honduras," Tony says rather directly. "We enjoyed listening to your stories."

"We enjoyed talking with you, too." With that Cassie sits back in her seat and opens a book. Max, meanwhile, continues reading his newspaper.

Twenty minutes later, Flight 544 finally approaches Louis Armstrong New Orleans International Airport. Stephanie feels a real buzz as she looks out the window and sees below the twin bridges over the Mississippi River and the Port of New Orleans with a row of cruise ships docked. She nudges Tony and nods toward the view. He looks out and laughs. "Seems like forever ago that we boarded the Swedish Gem and headed out to sea, doesn't it?

Stephanie's eyes well up with tears. "It's been an adventure, for sure," she sighs, "a week we'll never forget."

Tony closes his crossword puzzle book, puts his tray into the upright position, and reaches down for his carry-on bag sitting under the seat in front of him. He shoves the book and his pen in the side pocket. Stephanie uses the opportunity to rub the back of his neck. Her mind drifts to thoughts on what still faces her. She still owes Snake $15,000. She still has to make arrangements to have their belongings retrieved from the SCA headquarters in Miami. She still needs to decide where and when to tell Tony she is pregnant. And finally, she still needs to support Rachel. She begins to cry.

"Hey, Steph, what's wrong? Why are you crying?"

"Not now, Tony, I'm just tired, relieved, and I don't know what all. I'll be fine in a minute."

Tony kisses her on the cheek and pats her leg. He then lets her be.

The Super Dome and the Garden District pass below. The jet veers one last time on its final approach and in less than three minutes lands with a gentle jolt. Back safely in the USA, Stephanie and Tony feel a collective sense of relief as the usual de boarding rush plays out and they walk into the terminal. With only their carry-ons, they hustle through the bustling crowds to the nearest ground transportation exit. They hail a cab and quickly zip through the Jefferson Parish traffic onto I-10 on their way toward downtown New Orleans through the suburbs of Kenner and Metairie.

Twenty-five minutes later, the cab driver drops them off at the back side of the Julia Street parking lot where Tony's truck 'Smokey' has been safely and snuggly parked for a week. Tony pays the cab driver the fare plus a $10 tip. 'Smokey' sits on the other side of the fence less than 50 feet from where the cab driver dropped them off, but almost a city block from the nearest gate. Tony suggests Stephanie sit on the nearby bench while he hikes to the truck. She agrees and off he goes. It takes nearly 10 minutes for him to walk up and back.

"Hey, big guy," Stephanie says flirtingly to him as he stops at the fence, "for 20 bucks I can show you a good time."

Tony starts to climb the fence, but laughs so hard he nearly falls. "Maybe next time, but I will buy you dinner."

Stephanie blows him a kiss and shimmies her shoulders, "Sounds good."

Two minutes later he pulls up to the curb, "next stop, Drago's."

Relieved that Stephanie's mood has changed for the better they once again enjoy a cup of gumbo and a dozen char-grilled oysters, this time in a much quieter and much appreciated calm atmosphere.

Since their seven-day cruise abruptly ended on day three with Tony's Cozumel ploy, they didn't get to spend the week having casino time off and on every day filling the time among shore excursions, dinners, shows, and whatever else they would have done on the ship. Spending Saturday night at a New Orleans casino before driving home Sunday morning seems like a great idea. And so they do.

Stephanie heads for the table game pits. She gets wide-eyed over the variety of games available and the number of tables. From players hollering at the craps tables to the sounds of roulette wheels spinning, her adrenaline kicks in and she plops at the first open seat she finds, a Let It Ride table.

Tony heads for the poker room hoping to quickly get on a No Limit Texas Hold 'em table. He was not able to play poker on the cruise ship since not enough players signed up on the Sunday at sea day as the Gem sailed to its first port in Cozumel. He follows the signs to the poker room and sees an "open seat" on the board as he approaches. There are seven tables playing, four of them playing $1-$2 blinds, and three playing $2-$5 blinds. Tony hands the on-duty poker room host three crisps hundred dollar bills and kiddingly introduces himself, "Hi, my name is Open Seat."

"Nice to meet you Mr. Seat," the host laughs. "I see your name listed for table four."

The host hands Tony a tray holding $280 worth of red $5 chips and $20 worth of white $1 chips. The next two hours go by quickly as the eight players on table four all see their stacks of chips rise and fall with each winning a few hands and losing a few hands. Bantering and story-telling keep the atmosphere friendly. Stories flourish about everyone's experiences with this kind of hand, that kind of hand, how much won, how much lost, what came up on the flop, what came up on the river, and on and on. Each player tells his or her "I was this close to winning the bad beat" story, whether embellished or not.

Tony takes a much needed break after two hours of play. On his way to the men's room, he stops by the Let It Ride table to check on Stephanie. He does not get a happy report. "This is all I have left of $400." Stephanie shows Tony her only remaining seven $5 chips.

"Why don't you come play poker, then, if you aren't having any luck? There are some open seats in the room."

"I may just do that. Stop by on your way back. If I haven't won a hand by then, I'll go with you."

Stephanie does not win another hand by the time Tony returns. She grabs her remaining chips and goes to the poker room with him. Finding an open seat at one of the other tables, she hopes her luck changes. About the time she settles in, introduces herself to the other players at table two, receives her chips, and cards get dealt, a loud collective "ooh" emanates from table seven at the far end of the room.

George, a gentleman of few words wearing a black cowboy hat and sunglasses, has gone all in when the jack and queen of diamonds comes up on the flop to go along with his ace and ten of diamonds hole cards. Only one other player calls his bet, Riley, a young slightly overweight lady with dark hair who has been effectively using her push-up bra and low cut red sweater as a ploy all evening to her advantage. She has a pocket pair of jacks. Since both are all in and the only players in the hand the dealer gives the usual instruction, "Turn them over, let's see your cards."

The table goes abuzz when George shows his reason for going all in, a possible royal flush, and Riley shows why she quickly calls his bet, a possible four-of-a-kind. The dealer turns a harmless four of spades as the anticipation swells. The king of diamonds gives George a royal flush, the jack of diamonds gives Riley quads. The dealer turns over the river card, the three of clubs, and the moans begin.

The dealer pushes the nearly $1,000 pile of chips to Riley. George utters the ritualistic "good hand, young lady" sportsmanship response, even though he does slap the table hard. The other players quickly echo the comment as they watch Riley stack her winnings. Word spreads quickly across the room and instantly stories begin anew from players at every table about their similar big wins and near misses.

It takes three hands before Stephanie can chime in with her "bad beat" story. She rakes in her small pile of chips from winning a hand with only a pair of sixes, and uses the opportunity to tell the tale.

"About an hour into the first night I ever played a cash game at one of the casinos back home I had pocket kings and two aces came up on the flop. I bet $100 and everyone else folded except a guy named Snake who stared at me for what seemed like forever. He then raised the bet to $200. I winked at him and quickly called. A deuce came up on the turn so I bet $100 again. He called. When another ace came on the river I instantly went all in. I had just over $300 in chips. He called, and darned if he didn't flip over the fourth ace. I couldn't believe it. I was so convinced that my full house of aces over kings could not be beaten that it never occurred to me he could have that other ace."

"Learned a good lesson, missy, didn't you?" smiles Mr. Silverman, an elderly gentlemen across the table from Stephanie.

"He seldom talks, but when he does, you better listen," adds Jesse, another older gentleman regular who has something to say about just about everything and plays as loose as Mr. Silverman plays 'close to the vest.'

"What made it even more frustrating," Stephanie says a bit louder to make sure she can finish her story, "aces over kings full house wins the bad beat at the casino where I regularly play. You have to have at least quads, though, where I played that night."

"How much was the bad beat? Jesse asks.

"Just over $84,000."

"Oh my, now that's a story."

"Don't both cards have to play?" asks Mr. Silverman.

"Yes, they do," admits Stephanie. "You're right."

"Well, it's still quite a story," Jesse adds.

Almost in unison, every player at the table looks toward the big board on the wall watching the poker room messages scroll by on the bottom of the scene waiting for the one listing the bad beat. "$128, 147," Jesse says first. "Wow."

"It hit about six months ago for nearly a quarter of a million dollars," Mr. Silverman shares. As the next two hands play out, he quietly and slowly tells the story of that day.

"You've got to have at least quads here, too," Jesse adds to finish the story for Mr. Silverman.

All this brings back to the forefront Stephanie's debt to Snake and that despite safely being back in the USA and only an 11-hour drive tomorrow from home, formidable obstacles still lay ahead.

The bad beat doesn't happen very often, but just enough to keep players coming back day after day, week after week, and month after month to chase that jackpot. Just another of those "pie in the sky" fantasies that fuels the adult gaming habit, once less politically correct and more accurately known as gambling addiction. Just the idea of the loser of the qualifying hand getting half the jackpot amount, the winner of the hand getting a quarter of the jackpot amount, and the other quarter of the jackpot getting distributed among the other players at the table always keeps an edge to the game whenever the possibility looms.

The hands continue and by midnight Tony amasses a stack of over $800 in chips for his $300 buy in. He walks over to check on Stephanie when dealers change tables allowing about a 30-second break in the play. She has about the same size stack as Tony. "We need to head up to the room pretty soon," Tony tells her as he massages her shoulders. "We've got a long drive ahead of us in the morning."

"You're right. I'm ready whenever you are."

"I'm the big blind next hand," Tony says, "I'll play through the button and then cash in."

"Sounds good, so will I."

It's common courtesy for players to stay in the game, particularly if they've just won a big hand, and not leave the table until they play through the blinds. No "rules" require this behavior, nor do "guidelines" recommend it, but for regulars it tends to keep the games social over the long haul rather than too cut throat.

Tony plays his big blind hand, but to no avail as his suited six and seven do not pan out. He folds both his small blind and button hands, and cashes in with $780 worth of red chips.

Stephanie, however, gets a pocket pair of queens the hand before the big blind. She bets only $5 hoping everybody stays in to at least see the flop. Everybody does until the player next to her, a large man known only as Bud whose 4 XL t-shirt even fits tightly, raises the bet to $30.

Everybody else at the table folds except Mr. Silverman. He calls and shakily fumbles for his chips to toss in the pot. A "tell" Stephanie has picked up on, that usually indicates he's hoping to hit to make a hand.

The flop comes revealing a pair of fours and a queen. Stephanie's heart races a bit, but she calmly bets $30. Mr. Silverman again hesitates and shakily manages to get his chips into play. Bud decides to go all-in. He declares he has $740 in chips and shoves them across the line into play. As the dealer restacks them to verify the amount, Stephanie ponders whether to call him or not.

...Does he have the other queen? ...Does he have pocket fours or at least one four? ... Does he have two clubs with a flush draw since there are two clubs on the board?

Stephanie decides to call. Mr. Silverman casually folds. Everybody else shifts in their seats, leaning forward in anticipation of the showdown for a big pot. The dealer adds Stephanie's chips and tosses back only three after matching Bud's $780 bet. Over $1,600 worth of red chips now sit in a pile next to the dealer. Before the dealer can say anything, Bud and Stephanie toss their cards face-up onto the table for all to see. A sense of excitement builds among all the players as the dealer turns over an eight of clubs. Bud knows instantly he's on the verge of winning over a $1,600 pot if anything other than a queen comes up on the river. He, like everyone else at the table except Stephanie, wants a queen to hit.

Stephanie, so intent on trying to win the hand, potentially walking away with $1,600 or nothing, that she doesn't realize a whole lot more money is at stake. She neither hears the dealer when he proclaims, "Floor, potential bad beat," nor notices him as he gestures with both hands to remind the players to not mention anything that might disqualify the hand if the bad beat hits.

When the dealer turns over that fourth queen and Stephanie realizes she wins the hand, she feels a great sense of excitement. It's not nearly as much as Bud and the other players show. Bud starts beating his hands jubilantly on the table as the other players, including Mr. Silverman, jump out of their seats to let out a collective yell that can be heard throughout half the casino.

"Whoop, whoop," hollers Bud. "There it is! There it is!" Everybody else in the room senses from the yell what just happened. Tony runs over and sees it, too. He dodges past Bud who pushes his chair back enough so he can join in the celebration without having to get up, and gives Stephanie a big kiss.

She smiles and says quietly to Tony, "Gee, a $1,600 pot really cranks everyone up, doesn't it?"

He laughs. "The bad beat, honey, the bad beat, your quad queens beat Bud's quad fours."

It finally sinks in. Stephanie lets out a loud, "Holy shit."

She puts her hands over her mouth, starts shaking, backs up a step, and starts dancing. By this time a crowd gathers around the table as everybody within earshot wants to see the hands. There the cards sit majestically on the table; a pair of queens at Stephanie's seat, a pair of fours at Bud's seat and the flop in the middle of the table of a four, queen, four, eight, and QUEEN. A pile of chips sits next to the dealer which he keeps his eye on as the celebration continues.

By this time, the floor manager, a short curly-haired man named Presley who has mastered the art of spending as much time story-telling as keeping up with his duties, has made his way over to start the process of verifying the hand and keeping an eye on things as well.

A symphony of "How much does Bud get?" "How much does the lady get?" How much does each player at the table get?" fills the air.

Choruses of "At least $64,000." "Around $32,000." "Over $5,000 each." echo.

Cell phones capture the moment in videos, photos, and calls. More people from all over the casino crowd in. Stephanie and Bud accept high fives, knuckles, handshakes, and pats on the back as they stay in their seats according to the bad beat rules. The other players also stay seated at the table and revel in their instant bounty.

"Thirty-two thousand dollars," Stephanie says to Tony. "I just won 32 thousand dollars."

"I know, dear, I know."

"I just can't believe it."

"You better believe it," laughs Bud as he reaches over to hug Stephanie. "It's just as real as the $64,000 I'm getting."

Presley reminds all the players at the table to not wander away from their seats. "In fact," he says, "everybody needs to sit back down so surveillance can get a clear view of the cards and not see any behavior that they might question that could disqualify the hand."

About that time the shift manager arrives to start the paper work and gather IDs so payouts can occur as quickly as possible and the poker room can settle back into play. The dealer, according to protocol, leaves the played cards as they are, slowly suits up the entire deck, and then fans it across the table so the floor manager, shift manager, and surveillance can officially verify the authenticity of the outcome. The shift manager takes the completed forms and IDs to the nearest cashier's cage. Less than 30 minutes later, accompanied by two security guards, he returns to dole out the cash, $128,147 in total.

Presley, with the shift manager's permission, orders a bottle of champagne to be delivered to the table for the winners to enjoy and makes arrangements for Bud to have the penthouse suite for the rest of the weekend. He makes the same offer to Stephanie, but she turns it down since Tony and she are heading out in the morning anyway. "I'll take a rain check, though," she says.

"You got it," agrees Presley. "How about at least some chocolate-covered strawberries for the road?"

"You got it," agrees Stephanie.

In a few minutes the buzz subsides, and the poker room goes back to play as usual. As exciting and as unusual as winning the bad beat is, it does happen just enough to not create so much hoopla as to delay the action too long. The casino where Stephanie and Tony play most frequently back home, for example, opened its poker room less than a year and half ago. The bad beat has hit four times already in that span.

Stephanie and Tony finally get to their room a bit past 1:00 a.m. Realizing while she readies herself for bed, that she can now pay off both her debt to Snake and the bills for Rachel without having to dread teaching summer school, she gets a tingling sensation, partially from the champagne, and doesn't bother to put on her night gown. Instead she drops her panties, gives herself a good look in mirror, and scoots into bed. Knowing they need to get a few hours of rest before hitting the road home to Arkansas, she decides to give Tony the signal by kissing him on his ear while running her hand across his chest. Happy to oblige, they quietly make love and drift off to sleep.

14

Indeed, it has been a spring break like none other, but their adventure finally comes to an end. For the first time in nine days, Stephanie and Tony can relax knowing they had made it back safely to the states. They avoided calamity on both the Swedish Gem as well as the beaches and roads from Cozumel to Costa Maya and back up to Cancun. And most importantly, she can get out of debt … for now.

As they merge onto I-55 at the I-10 interchange on the western fringes of Lake Pontchartrain, they feel as elevated as the Interstate highway happy to be out of the New Orleans metropolitan area and on their way home.

Stephanie reminds Tony that she has only had her morning coffee and that a breakfast stop had better be happening soon.

"Watch for signs at the next couple of exits," Tony says to her. "Time for breakfast and a quick fill up of the gas tank now that we're out of the traffic."

With the prospect of "we made a baby" on her mind, something Stephanie sensed all week and unofficially confirmed yesterday morning with 'the kit,' she glances at Tony indicating her desire to get home as quickly as possible so she can tell him in just the right way at just the right time. She loads a Lynyrd Skynyrd CD and flips to song #14. By the time the second verse of *Free Bird* reaches its crescendo, Tony turns the volume all the way up to 30, head-banging to the beginning of the twin guitar solos, and shouts to Stephanie, "You know, '70s rock 'n roll, pretty-damned classic after all."

When the song finally ends and the volume turns down to a more normal level Stephanie punches Rachel's name on her cell phone contacts list anxious to talk with her big sister.

Rachel answers her phone and excitedly yells, "Stephanie, my dear little sister, how did the cruise go."

Stephanie begins to tell the tale of the past week, but Rachel can't help but interrupt. "Before you go on, Steph, I have to tell you something."

Stephanie instinctively anticipates the worse. "Oh no, Rach, what is it?"

"There you go another, Steph, also thinking the worst of me."

"Rachel, what is it?"

"I have made it past the first trimester of my latest pregnancy. The doctor says I'm finally going to have a baby."

"Oh my God, Rachel, this is incredible."

"I know, I know. How about that? Jimmy and I are so excited. Mom and Dad finally going to have a grandkid. What a hoot!"

Stephanie beams like a kid wanting to show off a new toy. She about bursts to keep from telling Rachel that she is pregnant, too. But, this is not the time nor the place nor the person who needs to hear the news first. Stephanie smiles at Tony and lets Rachel have her moment.

A few minutes later as they approach Hammond, Stephanie tells Rachel, "Got to go, sis, time to stop for breakfast. Talk to you later."

Stephanie and Tony eye the signs identifying the food, gas, and lodging opportunities available at the first Hammond exit.

"See anything good, Steph?"

One particular sign catches her eye. Stephanie puts down her phone and taps Tony on the shoulder. When he looks at her she raises her eyebrows, and with a sly smile, says something she has not said for years. "How does scattered, smothered, and covered sound to you?"

"Seriously … really … You want to eat at Waffle House?"

"Yeah, for some strange reason I just all of a sudden have a craving for it."

Epilogue

Tuesday morning finally arrives for Cooter and Hayes with Captain Gonzalez bidding them farewell by serving them a pot of hot coffee and a hot apple cinnamon burrito from Burritos Gorditos, a small restaurant known for its huge burritos about the size of a loaf of bread. "You will like this more than the watery oatmeal you've had all week."

Thirty minutes later Gonzalez sends them on their way with a simple, but serious warning, "I do not want to see you two hombres in here again, comprendes?"

They head for the port just in time to see passengers from three cruise ships disembarking. "Look at that," Cooter says. "Look at all the commotion here."

The whole area swarms with locals ready to meet, greet, and treat tourists to everything and anything designed to make their day so enjoyable that they'll want to come back again for more. "I'm telling you, we could make a fortune selling snow cones just to the kids. Look at all of them."

For the first time Hayes starts to see the potential. "You know, it might work. As hot as it gets here, it just might work."

"Yes, plus we won't have to face Snake," Cooter reminds him. "We'll be safe down here."

They walk across the main street to the entrance of the outdoor shopping mall and sit in in the shade for over an hour watching tourists come and go. With each passing moment, their enthusiasm for the idea grows. Finally, Hayes slaps his hands on his knees and stands up. He has a vision. "We'll build a stand right over there. People will pass it coming in and going out of the mall. We'll get rich. We'll call it *The Snake Pit."*

"Not funny, dude, not funny at all."

Special Thanks

To Arthur LeBon, Sherilyn Walton, and Dr. Kelly Jennings for their suggestions during the rewriting process; to Martin Briggs and Sgt. Paul Etzkorn for providing information about casino operations; and to the Norwegian Dawn security personnel for their information about cruise line protocols.

Read an excerpt from Tom's next two books

Redefining Moments:

Another Man's Truth

Harold and Louise knew that Evan would probably need heart surgery about the time of his 10th birthday. And he did, sort of. The first week of October 1962, just three weeks before his 10th birthday, Harold and Louise drove Evan to the children's hospital in the state capital for him to undergo a coronary catheterization. The procedure, as the seven doctors involved in conducting it explained, "Confirms the presence of a suspected heart ailment, quantifies the severity of it, seeks out the cause of symptoms, and determines the necessity of surgery."

No Cat Left Behind

A text message woke Sherilyn at 4:10 a.m. She nudged Tom next to her. "Good grief," she said, "there's another cat in the trap."

"Seriously," Tom mumbled. "I'm not getting up at this hour to go get it. Can't it wait?"

"Sure. The Humane Society doesn't open until 10 a.m. Go back to sleep."

Sherilyn replied to the text sent by Josh, one of the bicycle security officers at the Choctaw Casino/Hotel in Pocola, Oklahoma. "Which cat is it?"

"That black male interloper, and he's wild," Josh replied.

"Leave him alone," Sherilyn quickly sent. "Tom will be there later in the morning to pick him up."

"That makes 22 captured and only one to go." Tom yawned and went back to sleep.

CPSIA information can be obtained
at www.ICGtesting.com
Printed in the USA
FFOW05n0108311215

9 781634 910415